Rilke on Black

Ken Bruen

A complete catalogue record for this book can
be obtained from the British Library on request

The right of Ken Bruen to be identified as the author of
this work has been asserted by him in accordance with the
Copyright, Designs and Patents Act 1988

First published in 1996 by Serpent's Tail,
4 Blackstock Mews, London N4 2BT
website: www.serpentstail.com

First published in this 5-star edition in 2005

Printed by Mackays of Chatham, plc

10 9 8 7 6 5 4 3 2 1

Ken Bruen was born in Galway in 1951. The author of sixteen novels, he spent twenty-five years as an English teacher in Africa, Japan, South East Asia and South America. He now lives in Galway City with his wife and daughter. Serpent's Tail also publish *Her Last Call to Louis MacNeice*.

Praise for *Rilke on Black*

'The most startlingly original crime novel to emerge this decade' *GQ*

'The reading equivalent of a boxer's sharp jab to the solar plexus. It's fast-paced, tough, and pretty sexy' *Pulp*

'Boiled harder than salad eggs and much more likely to leave a nasty taste in your mouth' *Big Issue*

for

D

B

siempre

PART ONE

I'm not a criminal.

I've done my share of dodgy things but they managed to slide under the legal line. Then I kidnapped a man, a black man. Even criminals despise this branch of the business. It smacked of cowardice and worse, stupidity.

To add insult to cliché, I did it for a woman. I don't even think I liked her a whole lot but I sure adored her.

I was working as a bouncer. I didn't wake up one morning and think "I must become a bouncer." I didn't think God whispered it. But I sure look the part. I'm six foot, four inches, weigh sixteen stone and I look mean. Shee, I've behaved mean in my time but it's not part of my nature. It could have been as my father is a drunk. Always was. A very vicious drinker. Alcohol didn't turn him that way, it just fuelled the process. My mother lit out for Bradford when I was seven. That's where she probably still is and I reckon that's penance enough.

Dad was a Hitler. At fourteen I was big and most of all, I was ready. He slapped me in the face for some infringement of his manic code and I grabbed his wrist.

"It's over," I said. "Do that again and I'll kill you."

And it *was* over. The final slide for him had begun. He's a wino now. No frills or hard luck story, he lived bad and peaked. At the bottom of Shaftesbury Avenue, there's a small island surrounded by theatres. A drinking school have their patch close to the traffic. Maybe they like to hear it roar. Some days I think I'll have a stroll down that way. See what plays are on and see my old dad. As lead player on the island. No doubt he sings, dances and intimidates.

"The Old Connemara Shawl".

That was his favourite. I don't think I know another. So I visualise a visit there, surprise him mid-verse. Two solid fist blows to the side of his head will rattle some memories. It would not wipe out the years of waste but it certainly would feel fine.

I have a transit van. It looks like shit and I'm glad of that. Our local thieves have more taste. But wow, does it go. The engine is souped to an insane level and I've done a lot of work on it. I'd been doing "Moves and Removals" when I got the bouncer job. I met the owner in a Clapham pub. His club, Lights, was nearby. We'd fallen into one of those semi-friendly beer chats. He'd told me who he was and I'd told him precious little. He said, "My doorman got nicked today. Drops me right in it."

"That's a pisser."

"You look as if you could handle yourself. Done any of that kind of work?"

"Does it require a shit? As I've never done anything that needed that. I've done work that might have needed jail if that's any indication."

He gave a hearty laugh. The sort they teach you on nightclub trainee courses. It means only "Watch your Wallet".

"That's a plus right enough, in fact it should be compulsory . . . if you don't mind my saying so . . . and I

mean this in the best possible way, you look like a thug . . .
no offence."

I gave the laugh a try . . . and said, "None taken."

My nose looks broken, or as if it should have been. I
keep my hair cut real close to the skull and a dose of acne
left a riddled complexion. A nondescript mouth. That's
according to a woman I knew. I don't smile much. Thing
is, the true thugs I've run into smile all the time. I guess
'cos they know what's coming next.

I got the job and even worse the suit, a dress one at
that. A clip-on tie that comes off if grabbed. I was good.
I kept trouble to a minimum and hardly hit people. Rarely
hard at any rate.

I was polite and that in South-East London. That might
be the best arsenal of all. I don't have much schooling
but I'd been trying to educate myself.

The *Reader's Digest* . . . "Improve Your Word Power".

I'd sweated over that, chewing the words . . . fighting
the shame, clawing towards clarification. To my shame,
I'd begun to slip my vocabulary into use. Blame the
suit.

Until!

One evening a well-dressed couple tried to enter the
club. They were very pissed. But their accents . . . ah . . .
the BBC World Service. I was trying to explain it would
be better for them to call it a night. And I chanced the
description "inebriated". He laughed and she roared.

"Oh Gawd Cecil, is there anything more contemptible
than a chimpanzee in a suit trying to sound educated."

I might have let it go. Deep shame might have seen to
that. But he took a swing. I dropped him fast and took her

arm, whispered, "No darlin'... that's not contempt...
contemptible is to kick a man when he's down."

Then I force kicked him in the bollocks.

Dex is a psychopath. I read about that type in the *Reader's Digest* and he fits all the buttons. He lives across the road from me. Late one night after Lights I saved him from a beating. Outside his house two guys were raising welts on him. I stepped in and they took off. He said, "I owe you big guy, and Dexy always pays off."

As he brushed himself off I got a closer look. He was short and wiry, sandy hair and the face of a teenager ... he was thirty-eight then. Maybe boyish might apply but I don't think he was ever a boy. His eyes were grey and though they looked right at you, you felt they saw something entirely different. Not anything you'd want to see. I asked if he'd like a drink and we crossed over to my home. A one up, one down basic house with a basement. I keep my gym equipment there. I poured some Scotch and he got comfortable in my armchair, said, "Chez toi."

"Whatever."

"I'm Dexy ... after Dexy's Midnight Runners ... remember them?"

"Not off-hand."

"Big numero uno with 'C'mon Eileen'."

"Missed that one. You were in the band, is that it?"

"Hey big buddy, I don't reckon you miss much. Am I right ... am I on the old money there. Fuck no, I wasn't with the band, I used to take dexedrine, a lot of them evil suckers."

I nodded. Seemed he was still taking something fairly lethal. My measure perhaps. He drained the Scotch, held up the glass.

"Yo' partner. Hit me again with one of them piledrivers. So, have you got a handle, amigo?"

"Handle?"

"Yer name. Jeez ... what's this tight-mouthed act, fella? I ain't going to quote you, you can risk more than a monosyllable. Go for it guy, try one of them full sentences."

I didn't even have a twinge of irritation. I thought he wasn't firing on a full tank. I said, "Nick."

"Now that's a man's name. No friggin' frills. Just out and out plain label. How about I call you Nicky, how would that be?"

His accent was all over the shop. From American through plumminess to Irish. And always in the shadow of South-East London. I poured some more Scotch, said, "I'm too set in my ways to call a grown man 'Dexy' ... OK. So I'll settle for Dex and how about you call me the name I told you I had."

He gave a huge grin. Not a pretty sight.

"I like it ... yeah Nick and Dex the deadly duo. Sharp ... you're a sharp dude ... I can tell you'll need watching."

He leapt to his feet and patted his stomach.

"Not an ounce of fat ... I'm in shape old buddy."

I dunno if there's an answer to this but he was looking round the room. The pile of *Reader's Digest*s were painfully visible.

"Not a dentist are you Nick?"

Next he moved to the music system. I'd always planned on laying in some classical albums for show. Just go down to the market and buy a shit-load of culture. Mikados and stuff, fluff in some Concertinas and Allegros. What I had was Country and Western. An awful lot, a mini Nashville. I was beginning to gauge Dex a little and he didn't disappoint me. He gave a rebel yell and said, "I get it, you're a Rod-eoo star. Not the best town for it but I guess you took a wrong turn somewhere. No worries pal, I've taken a few of those myself."

He selected Reba McEntire and put her on . . . loud.

I said, "Why don't you just make yourself right at home, how would that be. Don't stand on ceremony."

Reba was bemoaning yet another done-her-wrong-man number.

Dex was wearing a light cotton suit. He flicked his hand against the jacket, said, "Sh-ee-it . . . I should be wearing Levi's . . . wow that bitch doesn't half whine eh? Now me, I like a blast of Heavy Metal. Give the old Metal to that dog eh . . ."

This was no surprise.

We finished the bottle and he told me he was a businessman. All of it seemed shady and risky. I don't imagine he'd have wanted it otherwise. That's how I got to meet him. We didn't ever become friends as Dex was incapable of that, but we saw each other a lot.

He fascinated me . . . and I think I amused him. Not from my wit but from his ribbing me. He liked to see how far he could push it and he was prepared to go as far as he could. I think Dex rose in the morning, opened his wardrobe and took whatever personality was current. Sometimes it fitted. Other times he was just dangerous.

He spent a lot of time at my place. I was never surprised to find him there, day or night. A Dobermann might have been better security but I'm willing to argue the point. A late Sunday morning, I was bleary eyed from rowdy crowds at the club. Feeling touchy as I'd had to hit a yuppie. Don't get me wrong. Sometimes a slap is the only reply but I didn't ever get to feel good about it. I was spooning instant into a mug and contemplating a second spoon to get in gear. Cold metal pushed hard below my left ear and Dex whispered, "Freeze mother-fuckhah."

I did.

Then he withdrew the pistol, laughed and said, "Had you going Nicky . . . you were shitting bricks . . . go on. Admit it."

My hands were trembling and it was a few moments before I could lay down the cup and spoon. I turned slowly. He was holding an automatic pistol and pointing it at me. He said, "Cat got your tongue?"

"Put down the gun, Dex, OK."

"But you haven't seen the best bit . . ." and he squeezed the trigger.

Banging on empty, six times and then it jammed. I swung with my left. The blow knocked him across the kitchen. The gun clattered across the floor and wedged beneath the fridge. I stood over him and a look, momentarily, of fear with rage filled his face . . . then it fled. For an instant the beast was exposed. I think I glimpsed the soul of hell itself.

My old man used to give me ferocious beatings. That's what I had intended for Dex but that look took it all away. Instead I said, "If you ever point a gun at me again, be sure of two things. One, that the gun is loaded, two . . . that you fully plan to use it."

He said, "Does this mean I have to make my own coffee?"

I left the pistol lying beneath the fridge. On ice so to speak.

A week later I was working when a cab pulled up outside the club. Three black women piled out and they were in hyper humour. Giggling, jostling, giving high fives. They were dressed for action with short skirts, sheer stockings and to me they appeared a jumble of desire. My mouth went dry.

All had pretty faces but the tallest of them was striking. As they approached I said, "It's the Three Degrees."

The tall one answered, "A white boy with a mouth. Yo' white boy, y'all gonna let us in yo' club?"

As I swept them in, she added in a posh voice, "Do pray tell us white boy, where you got your suit?"

I touched her arm lightly and said, "I'll tell you if we can come to a small arrangement."

Her accent reverted to sass.

"Wot arrangement that be white boy, wot can y'all do for little ol' Lisa. How that be . . . huh . . ."

"How it would be Lisa is, if you don't call me white boy, I won't call you nigger . . . how would that *suit y'all*?"

It seemed as if she might lash out but her eyes changed to devilry instead. Skipped inside. I've heard all that shit about a touch being electric. Hell, I've got Ann Murray belting out, "Touch me and I'm weak."

I believed none of it. What I learnt early was if you touch the wrong person, be prepared to lose the hand from the elbow. I lived on that preparation as second nature. Yet my fingers tingled where they'd held her arm. I shrugged and thought, "Time I got laid is all."

Midway throughout the evening, one of the staff brought me a glass of Guinness and said a customer had sent it with a message,

" 'Cos you like a touch of black."

I got involved in a fracas at closing so I didn't see the woman leave. You'll have noticed my use of fracas there. The study wasn't entirely wasted and it gives a hint of class to a punch up. When I'd changed, I got in my van and was revving the engine, just to feel the power. A tap at the window and there she was.

"What's a girl got to do for a lift around here?"

I thought she could do with coming down a notch but said wittily, "Climb in."

As she did, her skirt hiked up to her hips and I felt the stirrings. She smiled and said, "Gun it Bubba."

I thought of Bruce Springsteen's "Thunder Road":

> The door is open
> but the Ride
> it ain't free

"Where to?" I asked.

"High Street Kensington. Y'all want to help me lick some fish and chips?"

She can't have been more than twenty-five yet her eyes had the light of an old soul. Not a particularly com-passionate one. But they drew me. Her body was lush. I dunno any other word. It made me think of words like ripe, but mainly ravishment. As the engine kicked into gear, so did the sound system. Merle Haggard and his lonesome blues.

She lit a joint, held it deep and exclaimed, "Shit-kicker, music . . . the ol' Red Rock Call to Arms . . . Where's the white folk at . . . yahoo . . . let's go lynch us a darkie."

The gears ground in time to my teeth.

As we turned into High Street Ken, she said, "Ain't ya got no respect?"

That was it. I jammed on the brakes.

"Respect . . . you friggin talk about that and you smoke dope in my van without so much as a by-your-leave. You have some motor mouth lady."

She laughed.

"Whoa John-boy. I was meaning the music . . . don't you have any Aretha?"

God forgive me, I said, "Aretha Franklin."

"Oh no, Aretha O'Shea . . . get your head off yo' dick boy . . . there's a chip shop . . . my treat."

She jumped out and ran off. I turned off Merle and as if on cue, a cop appeared. I saw the panda car in my rear-view mirror. One got out and sauntered towards me, adjusting his cap. No doubt about it, the cops see too many cop shows. I let him do his finger number for me to roll down the window. What the hell I thought, it's his script.

"Would you like to alight from the vehicle, Sir."

Then we did the dance. Where had I come from, was the van licensed, insured, dry cleaned? All the rigmarole of polite intimidation.

We both knew our roles. I was nearly forty years old then and like the cliché goes, he looked about seventeen.

A spiteful nasty piece of work. Throw in the touch of power and you've got serious damage.

We'd come to the precipice part. Where he asks me to thin out my pockets and lets my property slip to the ground. I was just beginning to lose my place in the play when Lisa appeared. Her accent would have equalled Lady Di's.

"What on earth is going on here officer? What's your duty number? Does Chief Inspector Falls know you're harassing my removal firm?"

To me she said, "Walter, get the mobile and I'll phone the Chief Inspector at home, we'll get to the bottom of this immediately."

The old scalded-cat effect. Boy did the copper pull back, even removed his cap. I knew then why they sometimes call apologies "profuse". He was back in the panda and outa there in jig time. I don't even think he'd had time to notice that Lisa was black. She handed me a bundle of chips and vinegar. The smell you feel your childhood should have been.

As we got back in the van I said, "Chief Inspector Falls?"

"Oh, that was the first name that popped into my head . . . I nearly said Cloiseau."

"You mean there isn't such a person?"

"Oh, there's always a Chief Inspector Falls . . . only the name changes."

She held up a long chip and tilted her head back, let the vinegar drip into her mouth, then, slow, took the chip down, sucked and swallowed it. Turning to me she said, "I so like it slippery and wet, to tease a moment before I bite down."

"Where to?" I asked and tried to hide my physical reaction. I didn't know if her last description was a threat or an embellishment . . . I do know it sounded like heat.

She lived in Kensington Church Street and asked me in for a drink. The elevator was one of those narrow Gestapo jobs with a gate. It was a tight squeeze. How did I feel. I felt me all over her. She was smiling, said, "Remember that song 'If you don't know me by now'?"

Fairly heavy perspiration was rife on my forehead. She added, "You're probably thinking of that elevator scene from *Fatal Attraction.*"

Why deny it?

As we fumbled from the horror chamber she said, "It proves one thing."

I dreaded to know.

"What's that?"

"You white boys *is* smaller."

The apartment was like a shoot for *Roots*. I couldn't resist a Meryl Streep line . . . which I mangled, "And I remember, Africa."

She poured whiskies into heavy cut-glass tumblers and drank. She asked my name.

"Nick."

"Which rhymes with . . .? Let's see now."

I looked around the room at all the tribal artefacts and said, "Touching base with yer origins . . . is it?"

She leapt up.

"Yo' white boy, don't sass me, wot *chew* know about colour."

I finished my drink, said, "Listen lady. I've put up with your jive-arse shit all evening . . . yer street-cred rap and the knowing-hooker attitude. Wot do I know, you probably grew up in Milton Keynes. I grew up in Brixton, it's where I know and it's what I know. OK . . . you fucking got that soul sister?"

She moved right up to me, dropped to her knees and put her hand on my crotch.

"I'm going to blow you right back there baby."

I pushed her away, said, "I don't on a first date . . . can I use the bathroom?"

She recovered fast and said in a husky voice, "But of course, you run along and powder your tush."

The bathroom had every medication known to man. I checked my wallet and extracted a condom. Took ages to fit and I near did serious damage. I took a deep breath, said, "Let's rock and roll."

Outside the bathroom, I wrote down my address and phone number, handed them to her.

She said, "You think I wouldn't last spit time in Brixton?"

And she turned to walk away from me. I asked, "Remember that scene from *Basic Instinct*?"

And slammed her against the wall. I tore her tights and knickers down and pushed right into her. It didn't take long. As I zipped up she said, "Thanks for coming."

Outside I forego the lift and was heading for the stairs. A neighbour's door opened and an elderly lady looked out. The face of the perennial eavesdropper, the pinched eyes of the nosy-fuckin'-fucker. She said, "Nobody's in."

I said, "Oh, I've been in. I've definitely been that."

I wanted to leave Bonny out of this telling. But if I'm going to tell it all, then I can't omit her. She's the only person of warmth I've ever known. To have met even one might be bonus enough. I use a simple question about people, how do I feel after I've left their company. With Bonny it was always a warm feeling. She made me feel like the person I would have wanted to be.

I know who I am and, most vital, I know what I'm capable of. Bonny just shed light on other possibilities. I used to be a heavy gambler and a time there I hit a golden streak. I was following Pat Eddery and he was following the sun. I had wads, literal wedges of cash I didn't know what to do with. I gave up washing my shirts, I'd buy new ones. And not even look at the price. I bought a suit in Jermyn Street. So . . . I'm talking serious crazy money. Then it began to go wrong. And me and Pat lost our edge. Before I faded, I managed to get hold of my house in Clapham . . . and I hung Pat's picture in the toilet. I was going to print "Almost" beneath it but it smacked of melodrama and sourgrapes.

I was a little bitter though.

So so close.

There's a transport caff near by and I took to having late breakfast there. The owner was what they used to call a blousy woman.

Blonde.

Buxom.

Plump.

Near fifty.

But she had a wonderful laugh. Like Dyan Cannon.

The place was always packed. But my appearance usually gathered a space for me. Eventually it kinda got to be my seat. I always ordered the same.

Double egg over easy.

Black pudding.

2 sausages.

Bacon.

Tomatoes.

Thick white bread.

And lashings of tea.

The cholesterol nightmare . . . in neon.

Boy I enjoyed it.

One morning the owner pulled up a chair and said, "You eat as if you mean it."

"I do."

"I'm Bonny."

"What, by nature?"

A slow smile from her.

"Do you mind if I smoke?"

"Well, Bonny. I couldn't give a toss if you mainline heroin but I'd prefer you not to smoke across my food."

She held a cigarette mid air then tucked it behind her ear, said, "That's what they call clear and direct communication."

"Funny thing. They used to call it manners."

And we went from there. Got together twice a week and sometimes slept together. The sex was comfortable.

I didn't have to try and prove anything and she liked it enough not to analyse it.

She could drink and not get silly or is that vice versa. What I'm trying to say is, we had fun.

Then along came Lisa.

The day after our frisson in Kensington Church Street, I was in the bath when the doorbell rang. Throwing on an old robe, I stormed to the door. There she was in black leather pants and a red cotton jacket. A white T-shirt boasted her breasts. She was half pissed and looked at my robe.

"Fetching."

She told me to finish my bath and she'd make coffee. I'd just climbed in when she opened the door . . . and began to take her clothes off . . .

She had me in the bath
then on the floor
in the kitchen
and finally she had me exhausted.

I was lying on the floor reckoning I was going to die, just peg out there and then. At least I had washed for it.

She said, "Is that it?"

As I said, I'm near forty, I'm not able for these marathon sessions. I'm grateful for a shag and a sleep. But I was feeling smug . . . I felt I'd done brilliantly and oh mortification, I went looking for flattery.

"So how was it Lisa?"

"As I expected."

I sat up.

"What the fuck's that mean?"

She began to purr . . .

"Ah, baby, don't be sore, it's just you do it like a white boy."

I had to know. What white boy wouldn't?

"You want to explain that honey?"

"Mmmm . . . it's that you work at it baby, you try too hard . . . it's to be enjoyed, ravaged, celebrated. You make love with your head."

I got up and was too angry to reply. I was fumbling in the closet when I heard her say, "You must be the only man in London going *into* the closet."

Dex had left a six-pack of Budweiser in the fridge. He lived more in my house than I did. As long as he kept weapons to a minimum, I didn't worry. I noticed the pistol was no longer on ice.

I broke open a few Buds and wondered if I'd ever get it up again. Lisa had six months' worth in an afternoon. She emerged from the shower wet, said, "See I'm dripping."

The Bud I crushed in that manly fashion and grunted. Picture of macho bliss. She dropped herself on the couch, rummaged in her bag.

"Oh Nicky, I need you again. I'm weak fo' yo' sugar."

It would need more than a beer to get me going. I gave a playful shrug, not one of my better moments. She curled up close to me and held her fist under my nose. A soft sound like a bubble bursting plink and she jammed her hand under my nostrils.

"Amphy Nitrate baby, inhale deep."

And I did.

That was the beginning of all sorts of garbage. I didn't

slide gradually into usage and abuse, I plunged right in. She had her whole multi-coloured range.

Uppers.

Downers.

Sidewinders.

Ludes.

Speed.

Mellowers.

Jetters.

Black Kidders.

White Angels.

Shit, she had pills for when you didn't know how you felt. And even ones for when you most wanted to feel nothing.

She could get you:

Asleep.

High.

Awake.

Jittery.

Manic.

Giggly.

But what they mostly did, they got you:

Bad fucked.

And none came cheap. The reserves I had were hitting on panic. Worse, I was losing my edge. The one sure thing a bouncer needs to be is alert. I took a swipe at a customer and missed. He didn't. That was the end of my job. Lisa was delighted.

"You too good to be a doorman, yo' should be running yo' own place."

Jeez, I couldn't run a lighter.

"Lisa . . . I hate to kill the party but cash is running awful low, this shit's got to stop."

She pouted. I guess that can be sexy on some women. Me, I always found it irritating. She used her baby voice, "We going to have some serious money, Nicky."

"We're going to need it."

"I have a plan Nicky."

"And legal is it?"

She took my hands, gave me the earnest look.

"Baby, ain't nothing legal gonna give us fast and dirty money . . . you know that."

I could have stopped there. Before I heard a word. Kick her out. Clean up and get back on track. But I wanted her more than I wanted sanity or safety. So I said, "We're going to pedal dope, is that it?"

She ignored this, released my hands and began, "There's a black businessman, Ronald Baldwin. He started a club in Brixton called Rap. He's smart and ruthless. There are a chain of clubs now and he's into property and all sorts of shit. Then he got uppity, married some white bitch and got respectable. Are you getting the picture baby?"

I sighed.

"Old Ronnie's going to give us the cash, is that it? He's pissed off having too much."

She got excited.

"That's it baby, he sho' is going to give us the money. 'Cos we're gonna grab his black arse . . ."

"You're outa yer mind."

"No . . . no . . . no, he's a dumb fuck, he don't even have minders. We can take him easy."

"Dream on Lisa. You're way out there. This is never going to happen."

From then on, she never let up. A mixture of sex, dope and irritation eventually wore me down. My capitulation surprised neither of us.

"We're going to need a third man," I said.

She didn't like it. I could have cared less.

"But Nicky, that means less money."

"Money won't be the motivator for this guy."

"You have someone in mind?"

"Almost house trained. Certainly raring to go in some orbit."

I sure dialled the wrong number. Within five minutes they were matched. Dex's mix of accents and bile just blended right in with her rap and antics. I took off for the kitchen as they mixed street credits. A while on, Dex joined me, said, "You sly dog you."

"Am I to take it you approve?"

"Approve, jeez, I near came in my jockey shorts."

"Tone it down Dex."

"Whoops . . . sorry amigo. Your amour and all that. I got carried away. That is one *foxy* lady. What full-blooded male wouldn't put the pedal to the metal there, eh . . . Geez, the gazooms on her . . ."

"Hey!"

"Mea culpa . . . yeah . . . what is she . . . twenty . . . even that?"

"She's twenty-three."

"And you're . . . like forty . . . six . . . in there . . . am I in the ballpark?"

"You'll be on yer friggin' arse . . . I'm forty thereabouts."

"Like I figured, watch the old ticker my man. That babe's made for speed."

"You want to drop this Dex?"

I was close to dropping him ... especially as it was true. I pushed a coffee at him and drank from mine. It set the adrenaline and I tried to ignore my heart beat. Dex made a whooshing noise with his. A fun guy all told. He produced a silver hip flask, said, "See the ornamentation on there."

It looked like Arabic, very finely detailed. Old and too full.

"Nice."

"That's what you call it ... Nice ... it's a flamin' work of art. You need to get out them *Digests* again, you're pussy-drunk. Know what that inscription means?"

"No."

"Me neither ... fuck cares, eh. Am I right partner? It's got brandy, what else can us dudes ask? Say when."

He made as if to lace my coffee. I could have done with a healthy dollop but with Dex, who knew what else he'd added. I covered my coffee.

"Not just now Dex, it gives me a headache."

"Me too. That's why I do it."

Go figure, I thought. He drained his, belched and said in a husky voice, "Don't get up in a heap on me buddy but you're looking at bit peaky. Overdoing it just a tad I think ... are you eating right ... I mean, apart from the obvious?"

I wondered if a Dobermann mightn't be easier. At least I'd have some chance of seeing him coming. I said, "Let's get back to Lisa, she's got a proposition for you."

Good news for him as he said, "I do like me one of them."

Dex listened in silence as Lisa laid out the plan. From time to time he caught my eye and winked. This was indication of nothing. I'd bet he'd have behaved the same when told his parents were dead.

Lisa was convincing. Even I thought it might work. Concluding she asked, "What do you think?"

"I think I know him."

"What?"

"Yeah, I laid out a sweet deal for him once and he threw me out on my arse. Oh yeah, he called me a name I'd prefer not to have to say with a lady present. I can tell you later Nick but really, I'd rather not."

Lisa was on her feet.

"You're in then . . . you like the plan?"

Dex stretched back, deep concentration writ large, said, "Only one tiny quibble. One minor coddlywinkle . . . just the only thing I'd change, call me pernickety."

"What, what don't you like?"

"The part about keeping him in Nick's basement."

"What's the matter Dex. Want him to come stay at your house, is that it, that your problem?"

"Hell no, I say let's whack the fucker."

I gave Bonny a call. All I'd seen were Dex and Lisa and I needed out. I met her in the Rose and Crown on Clapham Common. A pub that still merits the name. The requirement was only to be a drinker.

You didn't have to play pool.

Munch Hawaiian crisps.

Play lotteries.

Be yuppified.

Flaunt on sexual prowess.

A pub. Bonny was behind a large gin on my arrival.

"Got off to a flyer," I said.

"It's the finish us ladies prefer."

I was drinking Scotch. Nice and easy. A vague mention was made of the new woman.

Bonny talked about the caff and the hassles, asked, "Do I smell of chips?"

"You smell good Bonny, and you know what? You look great."

"Not terrific?"

"Not yet."

But the night was young and I half believed I once was. Who knows how the mellowness might have progressed. Lisa's voice cut across this.

"So this is where you arse-skunk off to. A rendezvous with your old mum."

Lisa looked sixteen and I swear that was deliberate. Fresh scrubbed skin, extra-large baseball shirt and matching shorts. White knee-length socks.

The essence of jail bait. It had the desired effect. Bonny looked old and no one was more aware than her. I said shakily, "Lisa, this is my friend Bonny . . ."

"Oh my Gawd, I'm sorry . . . for thinking you were his mother. Oh please forgive me . . . let me get you a milk stout dear, I feel just terrible . . ."

Bonny got up.

"I was just leaving but I kept it warm for you. When you get to my age honey, you'll appreciate a bit of kindness."

As she got to the door, Lisa called out, "So sorry, but our babysitter will be waiting."

Without turning, Bonny shouted, "Ducks, I thought you were the babysitter!"

Lisa moved to finish Bonny's drink.

"Leave it," I said.

She did.

I could have pulled the plug. Perfect time to call it quits. But even then, fuming as I was, I wanted her. The more she riled me the more the physical attraction grew.

She glanced down at my lap, said, "I hope that's for me baby, not yer old mum's perogative."

Before I could answer, she put her hand on me, coo-ed, "Come for me sweetness, let that old tension go."

"Jeez," I said, "not here. This is my local."

"Come in your local," she whispered.

She stood up, said, "I'm going to run a bath, full of

bubbles. I hope you'll join me, we can just blow them ole bubbles together . . . don't be long baby."

I ordered a large Scotch. Such times I wished you could order a bath of booze. Climb in, open yer mouth and see fuckin' Katmandu. Escapism, jeez . . .

I should hope so. A guy moved up beside me. One of the staff from the nightclub, the glory days. I thought he might be called Jack. Not that I gave a tuppenny fuck either way.

"Yo' Nick! How you doing?"

"Hello Jack."

"It's Danny actually."

"Whatever."

"Man, I been watching you. What are you doing, interviewing the chicks now?"

"Hey, Jack. Let me give you a little tip. Nobody calls them chicks any more. It's not a great tip but you'll find it smooths areas of your life."

He thought about it. At least he gave the appearance of thought, said, "The old club just isn't the same since you left."

"I'll bet."

"So, are you working?"

"Yeah, on my tan." It was November.

"Where are you living now, Nick?"

I put down my drink, took a good long look. He didn't seem drunk. I gave a dramatic sigh, said, "What's with all the questions? You gave a flying fuck before? I don't think we ever even spoke. So how would this be, you fuck off back to where you were. If I need a reference I'll give you a call. Can you do that for me?"

It was time to haul arse. The bubbles would be cascading.

Two days later I went through the racing papers. I'm not superstitious, omens and the like I've never taken stock in. But a horse called "Lovely Lisa" was too much to ignore. Study made it even better, a horse on the make. Last time out, it seemed like it had been given a tug. The money hadn't been down I reckoned.

Alas, Pat Eddery was currently suspended. A relief perhaps as I didn't want to hold him responsible if . . . shit . . . I knew horses, this horse was due, this was a live one.

Deals with the devil. I'd already done that. Now I made my own deal. If this horse won, I was clear, Mr Baldwin wouldn't be in my basement. The old maxim, only bet what you can afford to lose.

"Bollocks," I said and upped the ante.

Part of it too, I dearly love to put the shite crossways in a bookie. It's a moment, close to sex.

The horse lost.

No long fandango of nearly or should have. Wasn't even close. Course I could have interpreted that as an omen all by itself. Now it was out of choices time: I tried telling myself I'd had the bookie going for a bit and that, sometimes, is as good as it gets.

I put the racing papers in the bin and wondered if they brought out any on kidnapping. Thing was, all the experts were in jail or highgate. The form figures weren't encouraging.

I got home, no cash to do a whole lot else. What I wanted was some quiet time. Just crawl into my room, close the door and howl.

Most of all, I didn't want to see or talk to anyone. As I opened the door, music nigh deafened me.

A figure in the middle of the room dressed in a ten-gallon hat, red-and-black shirt, black jeans, cowboy boots. Dex roared with the music: "I've got friends, in, low places."

He asked, "Guess who."

"Roy Rogers."

"It's Garth Brooks, the king of the shit-kickers, the biggest name in Country."

"That's *new* Country. I dunno that."

"Fuck's to know. They just added rock'n'roll to the old stuff. I thought you'd get a rise to this. You been a little down lately partner."

"Now I'm risin' . . . you wanna turn down the music?"

"But you and Garth, I thought he was a role model. The guy was a bouncer and get this, he met his wife through chucking her outa the club. Now is that not a Country song or wot."

"Thanks Dex, mebbe a little later . . . OK . . . now's not a real good time."

He flicked the hat across the room, said, "It's outa here. There's a big hit you should have a listen to sometime. Right up your street."

"Oh yeah, what's that then?"

As he stomped to the door, said, "Here's a quarter, call someone who cares."

Nice.

Once I read some lines from a guy who wrote them in the seventeenth century,

> By night
> we're hurled by dreams
> each one
> into a several world

> (Robert Herrick)

Got to tell you, he wrote it bang to rights. That's exactly how I felt and not just by night.

Silence. I couldn't even hear my breathing. Then the doorbell. Dex with one more adage. But he didn't stand on ceremony. Muttering, I threw it open.

Two young men in young suits. Hair as close cut as mine. They looked like the FBI or what they tell us these guys resemble. But in Clapham? One, or both said, "Sir, we are from the Church of Latter Day Saints. Might we have a moment of your time?"

Big Yank accents and attitudes to match.

I said, "Might I get a couple of bucks from you guys?"

"Sir, I'm not sure you understand."

"Sure I do but time is money and I'm a bit strapped. Caught me on a bad day."

"Sir, this is not our policy to . . ."

I cut him off. I was weary of the accent already.

"You guys really are *untouchable*. But so as you don't go away empty handed, we've got our very own Latter Day Saint and he lives right across the road. He'll be chuffed to see you guys. Tell him Garth sent you. Have a nice day now . . . here's a quarter . . ."

I felt better already. God works in mysterious ways OK.

If I knew Dex at all I'd be only mildly surprised to have him turn up late, wearing one of the suits. He already had their accent.

*

The kidnap strategy. Dex and I were going through it. I felt him eyeing me so I asked, "What?"

"How's it to be big?"

"Excuse me?"

"To be a large guy, built like a brick shit house."

Before I could answer, if such a thing were, he continued, "If I were built ... I'd spend the time cracking skulls."

"Jeez, what a thought. Don't you think you might tire of it?"

"Never, I'd never get tired of kickin' fuck outa them."

"Them?"

"You, the others. When you've got my shape, you've got to be quick and very very unexpected."

I laughed out loud.

"Rest easy Dex, you are both of those, in spadefuls."

"Speaking of spades. I see Miz Lisa has a whole new sparkle ... not knocked up is she?"

"Back off Dex. I don't need a taste of the qualities you work at."

He moved over to the sofa, stretched out and said in a quiet voice, "I'm going to tell you a story Nick."

"Don't feel you have to Dex."

"Just listen up, alright. I've always had a mouth. No, don't protest, I shout it off sometimes."

Then he stopped. I waited and he said, "Shit, wish I smoked, this is a story that needs an aura of nicotine. Well, we'll plough on. I was in a nightclub a few years back. I got into a beef with two guys ... two black guys. Words were spoken. Are you with me Nick?"

/

"I've got the drift."

But as James Joyce lamented, they weren't the right words.

"Fuck, I did my best but they didn't seem riled. Worse, I don't think they took me seriously. So I threw some money down in front of them and said, 'Hey, sorry about the hassle, have a bunch of bananas on me.'"

"Then I hope you left."

"I scored. Fuck-knows eh. A Chinese-American lady . . . or was she from Hackney? It's not relevant. I forgot about the apes."

"They didn't?"

"Wot, I told you this story already? I came out of the club, the lady on my arm, heavy sex on my mind, and this guy puts a knife in my heart. Now all I felt when I went down was 'Watcha wanna do that for?' The doctors said that you don't live if your heart gets touched. But here I am. Is that a Country song or wot?"

"And the moral?"

"Hey Nick, it's a story. Not a lesson. Your turn, amigo."

"For what?"

"For a story. Here's how it works. I'll tell one, your turn then. Thus we bond and grow to love each other over the camp-fire. Gottit?"

"I don't have stories."

"Sure you do, any yarn will do. Even a bouncing one."

"Nope, no story."

He hopped up and seemed genuinely disappointed. I knew I'd failed some bizarre test. He said, "You're a hard fucking trip man. But I promise you one thing. I down-right guarantee it. Before this whole deal is done, you'll have a story. Whether you fucking want it or not."

*

Lisa didn't show for two days. Then arrived, her eyes puffy. She'd been crying or getting high or both.

"Gimme a hug," she asked.

I'm a bit awkward at that spontaneity but I gave it a shot. She wasn't impressed.

"Call that a hug. Put yer pecker in it boy."

It didn't lead to sex. My fault. She got that look a women gets when they're going to put the rough questions.

"Why did you never marry, Nick?"

"I didn't plan not to, but one day I woke up to discover I was forty-two. It just got away from me. My career came first."

"What career?"

"Exactly."

"You could marry me baby."

"I could, but I won't."

She flared.

"You're such a sweet-talker Nicky. The old honeyed words. You could lie to me."

"Why?"

"It's called communication, to ease social interaction."

"No Lisa, it's called lying."

"Didn't you ever want to have children?"

"Nope."

"Never?"

"No."

That more or less put an end to that chat. I hadn't felt like explaining. How I was afraid I'd be my father if I had a child. With my luck, a boy would grow and give me beatings. A little girl, that was the worst scenario. I knew

I'd love her more than safety and she'd expose a vulnerability I couldn't bear.

Most times I barely took care of myself. Lisa crashed early and I put her to bed. She looked almost innocent as she slept. A time later she thrashed and shouted. Most of what she said was incomprehensible but I thought she called a name a few times.

It wasn't mine.

It sounded like Don... but I couldn't be sure. What was certain, she was far from pleased with him. Was it "Donny"... hardly Donny Osmond though that would explain the nightmare.

Come morning, I thought I'd lay on a treat. Set the table real nice, had coffee perked, toast heating and the smell of down-home bacon. Centre of the table one red rose. Water on its petals.

Just kidding about the rose. At seven in the morning, one flower is hard to come by in Clapham.

She liked it and after she said, "I want to tell you something."

I wanted to ask why everyone was suddenly telling me stories but decided to let it go. She began, "My mother was a lady of the night... well of any time. A hooker, or should I say prostitute. Ugly word isn't it?"

I thought so.

Lisa played around with a crust. Moved it back and forth on her greasy plate. Her voice lost all accent, inflexion... as if she was reading a script.

"Have you noticed all these syndromes recently? Everything's syndromised now. Perhaps I have PPSS. Wanna hazard a guess at that one?"

I could have made a reasonable shot but instinct said to

keep it locked down. This wasn't a scene for two players. I shook my head.

"Post Prostitution Stress Syndrome. Makes it sound almost respectable, yeah you could put it in a CV. Emma, that was my momma's name. She didn't know sheet about syndromes but she sure knew the book on stress. She used to say, 'If I have to see one more jonny fish, I'll vomit.' Cute name eh Nick . . . what she called a prick."

I definitely had nothing to say now. She continued, " 'I've seen hundreds of them and I've never seen one that looked nice' . . . that's what Emma said. Don't you think that's kinda sad, Nicky? Not one pretty prick in all her years."

I got up, made some fresh coffee. She wasn't finished though.

"She was a nice-looking woman, but by the time I was a teenager, she'd gone down the toilet and her clients got rough. They became more interested in me. You know what I'm saying Nick?"

I poured the coffee and knew too well. She caught my wrist.

"I got good at it Nick. Is this making you hot? Want me to be a little girl for you?"

I sat down and she released my wrist. I asked, "Where's your mother now?"

"Fuck knows. End of lesson."

I said, "It's my turn now, is that it?"

"For what? Rotating the chores?"

"I know how this works Lisa, you tell me a story . . . then I reciprocate and . . ."

"The fuck you talking about mister? You think I want to trade pieces of my momma for some of your memories?"

To my astonishment, tears were rolling down her face and she muttered, "You bastard, you jonny fish . . ."

They kept changing the rules. No sooner had I got a handle on the game, they moved the flaming goal posts.

Thing is, I did have a story: I wish now I'd told it to one of them. I dunno which would have understood the best . . . but I ought to have gone for it. Here's the story, less heralded now alas.

As a child in the beginning, I couldn't understand what they were saying to me. Then, I could understand but I didn't know how to respond. Finally, I could understand and reply and wanted to do neither.

Autograph books had a short burst of popularity in our neighbourhood, like hula hoops. Course, you could never get within spit of anyone famous so the book got full of bus conductors, milkmen, anyone who could write. My mother's sister had been good to me. Prevented my dad from thrashing me on more than a few occasions. She wrote in my book, "The cause of many a silent tear."

And broke my heart.

I grew up believing I'd hurt the only person ever to show me kindness. That weighed heavily on my soul and undoubtedly affected my behaviour. Only very recently, I'd found the book among old things. The pages were mildewed but legible. Who the fuck was Reg the Milkie or Tim the Postie. Christ they were nobodies then and not even remembered now. The Tab Hunters of Brixton I guess.

. . . and then.

My aunt's entry.

God in Heaven, I felt the blush of anguish, of early

shame. Then I noticed the very corner of the page was turned in. I straightened it and there was written:
... onions.

It took a moment for the penny to drop. She'd been joking, it was only a piece of humorous whimsy. So I had lived a large portion of my life on misunderstanding.

Well ... yes.

Have I thus learnt to look more carefully. Probably the result is that I check the corners first, long before I get to read the message. I know the Waltons would have liked this story which is verdict enough.

Lisa asked, "Can you trust Dex?"

"What? ... I thought you liked him."

"Jeez, wake up boy, I like Big Bird, you think I want him along on a kidnapping?"

"You get along like soul mates."

"Dex feeds me what I want ... myself. He's a mirror, reflects back the best of me."

She took her hand mirror from her bag, checked her face, said, "Dex is a type. Huge ego. Other people's feelings, thoughts don't touch him. He's not capable of love or remorse. His existence is based on other's weaknesses. The perfect urban predator."

"You've been reading my *Digest*."

"No Nick. Just surviving in London. See this mirror, turn it over and what is there? Just a black space. That's the very essence of Dex, it's a place where light has never reached and never will. The total absence."

"You're describing pure evil."

"No honey-chil'. You ain't listening. I just got dun telling you wot BLACK is. With your Dex, his tone, his voice, gesture, look like they change but it ain't nothing, it's empty. He be the hollow man Mr Tom Eliot look for."

"Or like in *Apocalypse Now*?"

"Yo', Nicky, don't try to mix references with me. Y'all pit cinema agin my readin'. When yo' gonna learn boy?"

Before I could reply to this attack she was off again.

"You watch TV Nick. You've heard of *Armed Response*. Bear it in mind baby."

"OK Lisa, I've listened to the lecture. Compelling it may be but it has one big flaw."

"What dat flaw?"

"Me. You said he reflects the other person. When he's with me, all he does it give me lip." She laughed out loud.

"Yo' Nicky. Planet Earth calling. Dat dee whole beauty of it. He give yo' back wot yo' most admire. Sass and savvy and right up to dee line he bring you. Sheet Nicky, dat where you live."

I replied pathetically, "That's not true."

"Oh, it's true baby, yo' know dat. In yo' heart, yo' know. When the time comes with dat Dex and dat time is surely coming. Yo' all distract that boy first. Get him go make coffee. Then yo' come up behind him quick and yo' cut dat mother-fuckhah's throat. Cut it full. Y'all hear what I'm saying?"

"Enough Lisa, you're losing it . . . I won't listen to any more of this garbage."

"Y'all heard me, I said – 'Full' . . . do it proper and do it proud."

That morning the phone rang early. Did I still have my van? Yup . . . wanna do a moving job . . . definitely. Would need two men. I told Lisa, she turned her head away, asked, "What colour are my eyes?"

"You're kidding me. It's seven in the morning and you're bringing me this."

I didn't know and she said, "You don't know."

"They're brown."

"Blue, with green flecks. Very striking."

"C'mon Lisa, what significance has it?"

"Oh nothing . . . if nothing's what you feel for a person."

"Gimme a break, OK."

"You won't know then what colour eyes Dex has got."

"I don't."

"Neither does he . . . have any colour. They are dead eyes."

"Lay off the poor hoor. I have to work with him today."

She concluded with, "The Sudi seek a joining of the mind and intuition which illuminates. This brings love."

"Yeah that too," I said.

Dex was pleased to join me in the day's work. He quickly changed into old jeans, work boots, plaid shirt and . . . I dunno where he got it . . . a white hard hat.

As he climbed into the van he was whistling "YMCA".

The job was in Camberwell and as I drove, he punched

my arm . . . in a friendly gesture. His accent sounded like
Jimmy Stewart.

"Gee Nick, this is great, us driving off to work, brothers-
in-arms. Buddies in the moving racket. Already Nick, I
feel very moved."

Another playful punch, a little harder.

"Gosh, ain't this swell. Dos honchos heading out
there . . . ARRIBA ZAPATA."

"Don't punch me again Dex, OK?"

"Gotcha. No punching . . . OK . . . how about heavy pet-
ting. Whoa, sorry big fella. Thing is, I love ya big guy,
that's the holy of it all."

He was silent a moment then, "Remember all those
buddy movies . . . two guys on the road. Scarecrow . . .
remember that, bet you like ol' Gene Hackman. No frills,
no shit kinda guy, yeah. You and me, we're like Kerouac
and Cassady. With Lisa as Maggie . . . whatcha fink
partner?"

"We're here. This is it."

An elderly lady was being moved into sheltered accom-
modation. A lot of her furniture was old and awkward.
As we manoeuvred items to the van, a teenager on a
skateboard whizzed right up to us . . . flip

turn

till his next run.

Dex said in a high cheerful voice, "Doesn't bother me . . .
bother you Nick?"

"No, we're nearly finished anyway."

"No one's bothered. Not even the old biddy who's losing
her home. It's a wonderful life."

We got the gear all locked down and I got back into the
van. Dex said, "Half a mo'."

He walked over to the kid. Threw up his right arm. The kid's eyes followed. Dex gave him an almighty kick between the legs. Then he picked up the skateboard and flung it back into the van.

I was too surprised to comment.

I put the van into gear and Dex said, "Weren't you just the teeniest . . . weeniest bit bothered?"

Dex launched into a quiet version of "I'm so lonesome I could cry."

Despite what I'd been thinking, I had to admit it was a very touching interpretation. Could have touched me if I let it.

I wouldn't.

I'd been thinking of the skateboard kid. I'd noticed he wore a grubby white T-shirt, with the inevitable logo and Americanese,

"Life SUCKS".

Well, now he had the experience to prove it. Without the skateboard, he'd be thrown back on the habitual frame of activity:

Phone kiosk destruction.

Glue sniffing.

And the nigh obligatory mugging.

Fourteen, or whatever he was. Already too old for crack dealing. I could give a fuck either way.

Dex said, "Lisa's mother's a teacher, right?"

"Wot?"

"Yeah, over in some posh school in Kensington."

"Near Kensington Church Street?"

"I think so . . . don't *you* know?"

Fuck on a bicycle.

We stopped at the Rose and Crown for the money.

Bill Shaw was waiting. He's so much a Londoner, it's near caricature.

> Loves his old mum.
> Loves his cuppa tea.
> Loves the Costa del Sol.
> Hates forgiveness.

He said, "You did a good job, mebbe we'll do more, eh Nick?"

"Sure Bill, anytime."

"OK, I better pay you. Take a cheque?"

Even Dex laughed at this.

I took the cash as Bill whispered, "No skin off my nose Nick and no offence meant . . . but I didn't know Dexy the Midnight Runner was yer mate."

I sighed. "There you go, what can I tell you."

"You keep yer glissy on that one Nick, there's a few dots off his dice."

"I'll bear it in mind."

"OK then, see you later. Say hello to the little woman."

"You betcha."

Dex and I moved to a table. He was loud grinding crisps, said, "Mmm . . . yum yum. Want some?"

"Can't you eat quieter?"

He gave a huge smile. Bits of crisp showed in his teeth.

"No can do. It's like sex, gotta be loud and dirty. But you're probably right to abstain."

I stopped sorting the money, said, "What's that supposed to mean?"

"Did you ever contemplate a diet? The old spare tyre's now suitable for a four-wheel drive . . . just skip a few dinners eh . . . say a big no to them burgers."

"Dex, you mentioned contemplation . . . yeah? Try contemplating this, how you'll manoeuvre a size fourteen shoe from yer arse. Here's your money."

He threw up his hands in mock horror, said, "No way effendi. I was honoured to be asked to share your toil. Let's not sully a noble enterprise with schetzkels. A bit of a drink on it for me is ample. Your company is my true wages."

"Well OK . . . but if you're sure."

"Aw fuckit, I'll take it."

And he did.

Then countered and said, "I think you're a little light here fella. Skimmed a wee tad too much from your fellow toiler."

"Fuck you."

He sat back, flicked a peanut in the air, threw back his head and

plonk,

right in his bloody mouth.

I'd prayed he'd miss. His reply as he straightened: "Now Nick-o, I'd dearly love to see you try."

Which endeavour he meant, we didn't specify.

I didn't ask Lisa about her mother. I had to button it down. I came close when out of nowhere she said, "If I had a baby, I'd call her Maria-Elena."

"Why?"

"After my mother."

"Didn't you say your mother . . ."

"What Nick . . . what about my mother?"

"I could have sworn you said she was a . . . an Emma."

"I never said that, you think I don't know my own mother's name. What is this?"

"Nothing . . . nothing at all."

And I hoped we'd leave it thus. But no. She asked, "The very worst thing a man can say to a woman, do you know what it is?"

I gave it some thought, then, "I've met someone else . . . and younger."

"Very good Nick, there's hope there. The worst thing is 'I understand how your ex felt.' "

"But I don't know your ex . . ."

"Woody Allen said he cheated on his metaphysics exam. He looked into the soul of the person next to him."

"Jeez, Lisa, is any of this connected? What's the point?"

"Poor dumb Nicky has to have it spelt out."

And she went, not quietly but hammerin' the door behind her. I shouted, "I'll miss you hon."

I resolved that come what may, no matter how I got round it, I was going to insert Woody Allen in my repartee. Nothing heavy, no big launch, just slip the sucker on in there, as if I'd only thought of it.

Annie Hall had been on TV recently and I'd identified with one particular line. Thus armed, I headed for a drink and some intellectual challenge.

As I closed my front door, Dex emerged from his house. He did what could only be called a pirouette and said, "Watcha think?"

"About metaphysics is it?"

"Eh? No, how do I look. I used our money from today. Barely made it 'cos of a certain shylock's shortchanging but quelle difference."

He pointed to his left ear. A single gold earring.

"You want the truth?"

"Naturellement."

"You look like an arsehole ... no, an arsehole with an earring."

"Hey Nicky, is that nice ... now come on."

"What can I tell you Dex. Only today I read it ... Life SUCKS."

I walked towards the Oval. Just pick any pub. I did, on the Stockwell side. This is where they mug Rottweilers. The place was having an identity crisis, twixt regular villains, motley yuppies and sundry. I guess I fit the third. A clean floor and dirty barman, but friendly.

I ordered a pint of Guinness and he gave it to me fast. So he wasn't Irish. No respect for the black.

Two stools down was a young punk girl. She had the

leather, chains, mohawk hair and gave me the fuck-every-thing look. I nodded.

Next thing, she moved behind me saying, "Can I sit next to you mistah?"

"Sure . . . yeah . . . OK."

She had a riot of make-up but beneath, barely sixteen. She said, "Do you ever wonder where all the stars went?"

"Wot, like Elvis?"

"No, real stars . . . my mum says the sky used to be full of 'em."

"She had a point, yer mum."

"Me fella's fooked off with Tracy."

"Tracy?"

"Yeah, she's like me best mate."

"Not any more I daresay."

"Not any more wot?"

"Oh just a touch of irony."

"Touch o' wot?"

I took a long swallow of the pint. Not bad. I wished she'd go away but here she was again.

"Wot are you mistah . . . fifty?"

"Not quite."

"Go on then, you look older than my dad, he's legged it 'n' all."

I wanted to say, "Surely it can't be yer personality the whole male population's fleeing from."

She nudged me.

"Wanna ride me mistah?"

"Wot?"

"You can . . . yer not so old . . ."

I got off my stool and gave her a direct look, said, "I'm

due back on Planet Earth as Woody Allen told Chris Walken."

I could hear her even after I got outside, "Woody who?" I'd say she's still there, the drone from hell in Stockwell. Jeez.

I'm dropping Woody.

I was soaking in the bath. At the stage where you think, "If I could only hold this moment I'd never ask for out again."

The phone went. It had that insistent whine that promises "Better answer me."

No Dex when you need him.

Muttering, "This better be damn fucking good," I dripped to answer it, said, "This better be good."

It was Lisa but I could barely hear her from deafening music in the background. She kept repeating ". . . what? What?"

So I lost it, roared, "Turn down the fuckin' racket!" She did then.

"No need to scream Nick, that's why we have phones."

"What was that awful music?"

"Awful! . . . he used to be with Bob Marley's band."

"Bob couldn't take it either, huh?"

"Don't be Redneck Nick, we can't all appreciate the nuances of Country music."

"*We* could try," I said. "All of us. Why are you calling me."

"To say I loved you."

"You're kidding, like the bloody Stevie Wonder song . . . I don't believe this."

"Nickolas, it's a spontaneous action to warm your heart."

"But not my bath I guess."

She sighed, said, "Elmore Leonard, you'd like him Nick, he wrote of Country music that if you play it backwards,

'You get your girl and truck back
You're not drunk anymore
and your hound dog's alive again.' "

"Cute," I said. She'd hung up.

I turned on the radio. What my old mum used to call the wireless. Kris Kristofferson was doing, "Sunday Morning Coming Down".

Is there a lonelier song, not that anyone could accuse him of singing. "And nothing short of dying/Quiet as lonesome as the sound."

I hummed along.

An ache nigh convulsed me. I knew it was bullshit and was missing something I'd never experienced.

It was like crying over a woman you'd never met. But crazy doesn't mean any less painful. I figured some dope would ease it . . . and did a few lines of coke. Let them good times roll, fuck-yeah.

I flicked the radio off and looked through Lisa's records. Bo Diddley? Yeah . . . my man.

The phone went. Dex.

"Amigo, I think it's time to wake up, smell some coffee. Know where I'm heading?"

"What happened to hello?"

"Hey Nicky, leave the humour to us better able, the strong silent shit suits you better."

"Was there something you wanted to tell me."

"Testy! Yeah, there's something . . . strap yer legs round this dance. Your chick knows Baldwin."

"What?"

"You heard. Guess she didn't tell you eh. Do I hear the soft sound of dee shit hitting the fan. Catch you later big guy."

My first impulse was to go direct to High Street Kensington. As soon as she'd opened the door, I'd bounce her across the hall. Used to be my job . . . But I phoned instead.

She was in the bath and half in the bag as her speech was very precise. Modulated, as if she knew slurring was but a word away. She asked, "Yo' baby, do I hear Bo in the background?"

"Fuck Bo."

"You wish . . . and me too I guess. I wish you were here in the bath with me. I'm all sudsy . . . and you're so hard baby."

Which was definitely a factor. But the coke was giving me an icy concentration that would evaporate in seconds. I had to cut through the smoke screen.

"You know Baldwin."

"Who?"

"For fucksake Lisa, the guy we're going to snatch."

I expected denial. What I got was purring. I dunno if you can slur that but she was close.

"Don't be mean to me baby . . . y'all come on over and let me stroke yah."

The coke moved into overdrive. The kill before the burnout.

"How many of us were you planning to service, is Baldwin invited too?"

The line went dead and my high and my dick. A depression moved right in to fill the vacant lot. I wanted to hurt somebody, anybody. The idea of crossing over to Dex and kicking the shit outa him was powerful.

The phone rang. Sliced across my fried brain. She launched right into it.

"I worked for him at his first club. A long time ago. How do you think I know so much about the dude? What, 'cos he's coloured, you think I found him in the yallah pages. Listed under kidnap possibilities. Don't be jealous baby . . . don't be jealous honey-chile . . . I'll come over and lick it better."

"Why didn't you tell me, eh?"

"I was afraid darlin', you so big, yo' so well hung."

"Cut the crap sister. Put yer act together by this evening."

"I'll be there baby. I'll be there for you."

I could have walked then. Pull a righteous indignation act and split. For one glorious brief moment I thought and roared . . . "FUCKEMALL."

I went rummaging in the cupboard to see if Lisa had left any other chemicals. Found some white powder and hoping to hell and gone it wasn't talc, I snorted deep. Nothing for a few moments.

"Bummer," I said.

Then a massive rush. What a coronary must be like. My nose was corroded as if red hot peppers were running riot.

Not coke.
          Not talc
but friggin methedrine.

A cold sweat leaped all over my body. I was leaking chills. I had a ferocious compulsion to smoke about nine cigarettes. Why that number I dunno but it seemed to make perfect sense. A cascade of noise in my head. Strung out thus, hours went by.

At one stage I tried to read, thinking words would calm me. I had collected a diverse collection of articles culled from my *Digests* on every subject. All in that quest for vocabulary. Among these were some letters William Burroughs had written to Allen Ginsberg.

Thinking the literature of drugs was appropriate or should that be vice versa?

Never no mind. This is what I read: "I was first arrested when I beached, a balsa raft suspect to have floated up from Peru with a young boy and a toothbrush. (I travel light, only the essentials.)"

This wasn't doing me a whole lot of good but it's hardly fair to blame Burroughs.

More: "One night, after shooting six ampoules of dolophine, the ex-captain found me sitting stark naked in the hall on the toilet seat (which I had wrenched from its moorings) playing in a bucket of water and singing 'Deep in the Heart of Texas'.

"At the same time complaining, in clearly enunciated tones, of the high cost of living."

Two things I realised I didn't know after I read this. What the hell were dolophines and, maybe more important, what were the words of "Heart of Texas"?

Food . . . yeah, I could eat. Perhaps that would ease me

on down. I wanted warmth too . . . the Bonny brand. Some
sort of sanity was essential, nigh vital.

"You look like shit," Bonny said.

"This is hello?"

The rush-hour manic food crowd had gone. Grease hung in the air and a breath-gasping pung of vinegar ruled. She was drinking tea. A pack of Marlboro lights before her. I leant over and took one.

"What are you doing?"

"Borrowing one of your cigarettes. Why you won't buy mule kickers and be honest is beyond me. Marlboro lights for fucksakes. Why . . . you mind?"

She looked as if she minded a lot. A cigarette?

Deep sigh from her. Worse, it had a horrible lilt of understanding in there. True sickener. She said, "You'll walk in here tomorrow and say—'Here's that cigarette I owe you'— is that how it'll work? I thought you quit."

"What's this, you're my mother now . . . what do you care? . . . here, keep the bloody thing."

And I crumpled it, threw it on the table. It curled there like a sad dream. Stood up and went to the vending machine, praying I had change.

I did.

Bought a pack with health warnings so heavy on it that it throbbed in my fist. Sitting back down I felt like a horse's arse. Made a childish display of "borrowing" her lighter and lighting up.

All the time she just watched me. Vintage Bonny. Let you jump in with both feet. I drew heavy on the cigarette and it tasted like stale manure. But I had to stay with it. I dunno what flavour I was expecting ... not hope anyway!

Bonny reached over, took my hand. She had green eyes but I didn't think I'd tell Lisa. A faint aroma of chips around her. A comforting aroma of false childhood was mixed in there somehow.

"Nick, what's going on? You're going to hell in a bucket. Is it money? I do know it's the woman but there's nothing I can do about that. You'll take it all the way to burn out. But I can help financially."

"Yeah, it's cash."

"What do you need?"

"How does five hundred sound?"

Sounded harsh is what it did. Her face gave only a tiny moment of hesitancy, then she said, "OK ... give me a few seconds."

What the fuck I thought. In a short while, I'll be getting half a million and I'll treat her proper. She returned and gave me a soiled envelope, felt solid. The voltage that money gives. I whispered, "Pat Eddery."

"What?"

"Nothing, just an old memory."

PART TWO

"A man's dress tells you what he does"

Ecclesiastics 19:27

How to tog out for a kidnapping. Dex was wearing a green combat jacket, black combat boots and dirty blue jeans. He asked, "Recognise the look?"

"Early evening wino?"

"Mickey Rourke in *A Prayer for the Dying*."

"Missed that."

"And a whole lot else besides."

I was wearing trainers, grey sweat shirt and jeans. The urge to dress entirely in black I'd suppressed. It wasn't a night for overstatement. Least not yet.

We were parked outside Baldwin's club in Brixton. Lisa had already gone in. One o'clock in the morning and the streets were hopping. If Lisa was right, Baldwin left at the same time without fail. Dex had produced some animal tranquilliser which now rested in Lisa's bag. She measured the dose and provided the syringe.

I'd worried. "Is it safe?"

"Well baby, the animals haven't complained."

Needless to say, Dex got a kick outa that.

I persisted. "We don't want to kill him do we?"

Dex smiled, said, "Some of us don't."

Like so many things, I let it slide. A flurry of giggling

girls passed. A batch of teasing innuendo. Youth and hope. I thought I couldn't recall either. Dex said, "You can get a virgin to sit on your face for seven bucks."

"What?"

"Jimmy Woods in *Salvador*. You've got to get past *I Love Lucy* re-runs. Hate to be Mr Deeds but you're cinematically illiterate. Fuck, you're bordering on ignoramus."

I gave him the look. He tapped his watch.

"Crying-time."

I didn't wish him luck. As it wasn't that kind of business. Plus, I didn't want to. I watched him join the crowds. Thing was, he did look like Mickey Rourke. But late-night Brixton, most do, even the women. Then I could see Lisa. No sign of Baldwin. His boast was, according to Lisa, "In Brixton, I don't need protection. I am the protection."

Nice foolish ring to it. We were about to test the theory. Was hoping they'd fail. From there maybe I could begin to crawl back. A rap on the side of the van. I jumped out. Lisa and Dex were supporting what appeared to be a very drunk man.

"Wake up Nick, open the back doors for fucksake."

I did.

They threw him in, I had a glimpse of an Armani suit and hand-tooled shoes. He seemed tiny. Lisa came up front with me. She was in high excitement and her breathing near choked with adrenaline.

"I bopped him that needle right in the club, he never felt it. I thought it wasn't going to work. Then when he got outside, he just folded. His fuckin' legs just buckled. Awesome . . . so watcha staring at . . . drive this fooker . . . let's boogie."

As I pulled out, I checked Dex in the mirror. He was going through Baldwin's pockets and none too gently.

"Cut that out," I shouted.

He didn't and held up a black wallet. A confetti of plastic began to pour out. Dex said, "Friggin' credit cards, wot happened to cash you black fuck?"

He turned to look at me. It was tight for space back there but he was near his full height. His tight work boot shot out and belted into Baldwin's head.

I jammed on the brakes. Lisa grabbed my arm and I shook her off. Climbed over the seat. Dex had fallen off balance and as he rose I hit him with everything I had.

Dazed for a few minutes he then put his hand to stem the blood from his nose, he gave a weak snigger, asked, "The fuck you do that for?"

"No pain, no gain."

"Wot?"

"Freddy Kreuger. *Nightmare on Elm Street*. Literate enough for you?"

I'd prepared the basement. How pleased Bonny would be at what her money provided.

A thick chain fixed to the wall to be attached to Baldwin's ankle. The prisoner of Clapham. Christ it made me want to puke even to look at it. To chain a human being, something in you has to be extinguished. You douse a light that can never be re-lit.

An army cot I got on the Walworth Road for a tenner. I went to Oxfam for the lamp. It had a shade with small cute mice playing guitars. He was sure to love this. It had certainly been a hit with Dex who said, "What age exactly do you think he is . . . ten mebbe?"

I'd laid in ten cans of purdey. With the onslaught of designer waters, this had joined the range of healthy beverages.

Truth be told, I liked the can. It contained:

Vitamins.

Herbs.

Ginseng.

I thought it might keep him healthy.

I didn't know if he was a reader or not . . . and if so . . . what. Some James Baldwin or Chester Himes . . . or Walter Mosley. What? I hadn't the courage to leave my *Reader's Digest*s. All the abuse I was going to take for them I'd already taken. Some copies of *Ebony*.

A cheap walkman as music would pass the time for him. Then a new dilemma.

What tapes would he like? From the sublime to the ridiculous. I got Aretha and Whitney Houston. I drew the line at Stevie Wonder. Not even a hostage would endure that torture.

Then I thought . . .

"Whoa . . . hold the goddamn phones. What am I doing? This is some house guest. Who gives a toss what he likes? I mean . . . wot . . . he's going to leave 'cos he doesn't like Whitney Houston?"

Was I losing it big time or wot? Did I expect the good kidnapper of the year award or wot?

To get some background, I thought I'd read up on captivity. Nothing could get me to concentrate on Patty Hearst. I just didn't possess that degree of masochism. Or the heavy-weights, like Waite, McCarthy. Too much

dignity and nobility these. Was I going to rub my own
nose in it. A gallop towards the classics was equally fruit-
less. Robert Louis Stevenson just didn't seem to jell with
the climate of Clapham.

"Fuck," I said, "I'll wing it. How difficult can it be?"

Chain a man, threaten him, intimidate his wife ...
collect the ransom ... ride off into a Brixton sunset.

Piece of cake.

Dex had tried giving me instructions on dealing with
Baldwin. At all times we'd be masked. None of these
heavy balaclava yokes or the sweat-inducing ski jobs.
Lisa had made light cotton ones. The sort of thing the
Klan might have for those long balmy Southern evenings.
Dex said, "We've got to give a lot of red herrings ... use
an accent Nick, can you do Irish?"

"This isn't Vaudeville, for fucksake. Not even the
Irish do it with any conviction any more. Do us a bleedin'
favour."

Another theory was for me to have an obvious tattoo
he'd remember.

"Tattoo yourself, Dex ... OK ..."

I did go along with leaving some envelopes in among
the pages of the magazines. These were pinched at
random from North London houses.

As we'd argued back and forth over these various diver-
sions, Dex had thrown his hands in the air and shouted,
"None of this would be necessary if we just put the bastard's lights out."

And Lisa had given me that look that said, "See!"

My street was quiet and we bundled him into the house.

The four of us linked in drunken bonhomie apparently. The animal tranquilliser and Dex's boot had done their work. Baldwin was out cold.

I laid him on the cot and fixed the chain to his ankle. Then I stood looking down. A quiet "sploosh" put my heart pounding. Dex had helped himself to a can of purdey. I said, "The fuck you doing, they're for Baldwin."

"He's going to notice one's missing. Take it outa my share . . . Slainte . . . that's Irish for Cheers. Tell you wot though, the fuck doesn't look much lying there. Not so high and mighty now."

Sweat was cascading down me. God I needed a drink. Lisa turned to me. "Go get yourself a drink baby, I'll stay here."

I looked at Dex, said, "You come with me."

He snapped his heels together, threw a Hitler salute, shouted, "Yaboob Herr Kommandanten."

In the kitchen I cracked open a bottle of Scotch and drank it by the neck. It burned like desolation and I wanted that.

Dex moved in close. "Tell you big guy, we should have gone for them with a tattoo. Truman Capote knew a lot of the heavy killers on Death Row. Their common characteristic was a tattoo."

I didn't answer. Trying to keep the Scotch down. It settles poorly on bile. He continued, "How much notice can you take of a faggot eh?"

"Baldwin's a homosexual?"

"Jeez, pay attention. Truman Capote. When he was in Russia he flounced out of a hotel in high camp. Swishing it up in front of the comrades. An American official tried to apologise to the Russkies. And the Russkie smiled, said 'Oh we've got them here but we keep them chained.' "

"You like that Dex, don't you. How long have you had to hold it until the suitable moment arose?"

What I really wanted to ask but I heard horrible echoes of that punk in Stockwell, was, "Truman who . . ."

I had half the Scotch gone and couldn't feel it. What I could feel was the sensation of locking the chain on Baldwin. He had a small skinny ankle and I doubt I ever saw anything as vulnerable. One more image to add to the shit heap. I didn't catch what Dex was saying.

"I didn't catch that Dex, run it by me again."

"I asked if I could have a drink too. That purdey is vile shit, must be good for you."

I handed him the bottle. He took out his hankie. Being Dex, it was more yer red bandanna, from his country personality no doubt. Slowly he made a big production of wiping, holding up to the light and closely inspecting the neck of the bottle, said, "No offence buddy."

"Keep it yer nasty fuck, just keep putting it in my face."

"Lighten up, amigo, we're all under a lotta pressure. Lose it here and you're in a world of hurt . . . 'Predator' . . . I'm just joshing you, nothing meant."

I snapped the bottle off him.

"Get yer own fuckin' drink and get the fuck outa my way."

He danced nimbly to the side. I headed back to the dungeon. Baldwin was naked on the cot, like a wizened golliwog. I stormed to Lisa, "What on earth are you doing . . . are you planning to mount him or something?"

"Baby . . . baby, cool it . . . I had to get his underpants."

"What . . . what kind of shit are you and Dex taking . . . and can I plu-eez have some soon?"

"Sh-ss-ish darlin', it's to send to his wife . . . unless you want me to sent an actual part of him . . . do you . . . do you want to slice him . . . is that it? Like to carve some dark meat?"

"Course I don't want it . . . hey back off alright. Gimme some fuckin' room. I just want to know what's happening BEFOREHAND. Enough with the surprises, alright?"

"Whatever you say, baby . . . yo' the man."

"Hey, could you stop with that baby shit. I can't tell you how fuckin' irritating it is."

She didn't like it and I could give a flying fuck. I was on the verge of walloping the be-japers out of her . . . and Dex.

She held up the underpants. I could see the brand. Calvin Klein. Another guy who'd had a kick in the head.

She said, "We've a call to make."

Upstairs, Dex was stretched on the sofa. He'd changed his outfit. Unbelievably for him he was wearing a garish-coloured kimono but worse, he'd brought the cowboy boots. Very elaborate black jobs with the high stitching, I could see his bare legs, white and absolutely hairless. Like sick alabaster, like a corpse. I felt a chill. The boots were plonked on the arm of the sofa. Apparently engrossed in a copy of *Ebony*, he didn't look up. I slapped them off.

"Get 'em off the furniture."

"Testy," he sighed.

Lisa produced a large padded envelope and put the

underpants inside. Dex gave a huge chuckle, said, "You're going to have to stop writing to Tom Jones."

She ignored him, wrote an address. Then she moved to the phone.

"You know what you're going to say?" I asked.

Dumb right but I was puke nervous.

"No Nick, I'm going to chat about the weather."

Like I said, dumb.

She sighed for quiet. Dex mimicked pulling a zip across his mouth. He looked like an evil child.

Lisa was talking.

"Mrs Baldwin . . . Mrs Ronald Baldwin, so sorry to trouble you at this latish hour but glad I caught you home . . . We took your hubby tonight . . . no this is not a poor idea of a joke . . . yes, I am aware of the time. Time for you to listen up . . . kidnapped . . . yes . . . ugly work but fitting . . . you hang up and his balls are in the next post . . . put you right off your grapefruit segments . . . That's better . . . Don't swear at me you white bitch . . . you get him back for one and a half million. I perfectly serious . . . so sell the family jewellery . . . I could give a fuck, sell yisself . . . Be home at eight tomorrow evening . . . you'll have proof . . . as they say 'The cheque's in the mail' . . . a little Calvin Klein reminder . . . no, he's not hurt, not yet. Y'all have a good night now . . . Bye now, tootle pip."

I'd never seen Lisa sweat, not even in the wildest lovemaking . . . she was sweating now, and speeding. She gasped, "Christ, wot a rush. Better than sex. What's with the look Nicky . . . you could hear? She sassed me, tried to be uppity."

"Nice going Lisa . . . especially the bit where you called

her a *white* bitch. How hard it's gonna be to figure your tint."

"So wot . . . as long as she pays."

"It's careless is what it is."

Dex watched back and forth, like Wimbledon. Hard to say who was winning. Lisa shrugged and went upstairs. He raised an eyebrow. I wanted to go to pieces as fatigue washed over me. Dex said, "Night John-boy."

I had some brilliant wipe-out remark in preparation but sleep got me first.

"One too many mornings, and a thousand miles behind . . ."

Which is about where I felt when I woke. First thing I noticed were Dex's boots. Standing alone and evenly lined up, like a tiny forlorn salute.

I thought he was watching me as his eyes were open. But it wasn't me. A look of nothingness . . . not blankness, just nothing. A face that had never retained the mark of a single experience or emotion. The eyes frozen.

I'd tried to figure what lay behind the multi personas. As I realised Lisa was right, I felt the chill along my back. I didn't want to be the first thing those eyes looked on as the face began its routine of movement, adapting to whatever personality the mind seized. Slipping past him I went to the kitchen. Made me an elephant coffee. I didn't want a hit of caffeine. It was blitzkrieg.

When it makes you want to throw up, you've got the combo. I knew there'd be a lot more unpalatable things these next few days. The coffee didn't make me feel better. Hell-no, it just woke me enough.

I was heading for the basement when I remembered the flaming mask. I pulled it on and checked in the mirror. I looked like a terrorist with a hangover. Aloud I said, "Horse's arse."

*

Baldwin was sitting on the cot, supping from a can of purdey. He watched me approach. I knew he was in his sixties and he certainly looked it. If a black person can have a black pallor, he'd achieved it. Naked except for a blanket . . . and the chain . . . he looked pathetic. I know now what woesome means. Till you saw his eyes. Jumping with intelligence, you knew this one was a sharp cookie. He said, "Dr Livingstone, I presume."

Then he rattled his chain and added, "By the rattling of my chains, something foul this way comes."

The BBC must have loved his accent.

Neutral.

Clear.

Concise.

Polished.

Modulated.

All the friggin' things mine wasn't. I was south of the river, always would be. An accent like his could convey effortless intimidation. In my corner I had size on my side and it was time to flex it.

Baldwin was about five foot, five inches and looked shorter. A black gnome with bright eyes, looked on me. I hunkered down beside him and began, "You know what this is . . . what's going down here."

"It's downright stupid, I know that."

I gave him a slap to the side of the head. The eyes burned.

"Whoa . . . little guy, lose the attitude . . . OK. Let's get that squared away from the off. See my size . . . and you just learned I'm a mean fuck. You do what you're told, button yer lip... we get paid... you're outa here. Simple."

"How much will you demand?"

"One and a half million."

He gave a huge laugh so I slapped him again. A degree harder.

"What's the joke?"

"You haven't a prayer."

"You best pray, fella. The rest of the team, they make me look like the good guy."

I raised my hand and he ducked.

"See, you're getting the picture already."

I prepared a fry-up for his breakfast. Heavy on the eggs. By the time I switched them from the pan to the plate, they were a mess. The toast was black. A sort of pathetic fallacy according to the *Digest*. Was he a tea drinker? Not any more. What we stocked was coffee, all the current residents being wired. Lisa had laid in one carton of fresh juice. I had a glass and only then realised how adrenaline had dehydrated me. Jeez, it tasted good, walloped in another. Ah... there was a quarter of a glass finally for him. Captives can't be choosers.

Back on with the mask again and serious irritation. I found an old track suit and brought it along.

As I set the tray before him, I asked, "You're name's Ronald, right... so I guess I'll call you Ronnie."

"No one calls me that... ever."

"They do now... here's something for you to wear and your breakfast. Hope you like eggs."

I had to unchain him to get the tracksuit on but he

didn't struggle. With a disgusted sound he stirred the food.

"I don't eat cholesterol."

"Then you don't eat."

"No tea."

"Right."

"Too much to hope for decaffeinated, I suppose. Tad tight with the juice. Budget a shade low perhaps?"

I pointed with my hand.

"You got music, stuff to read. Could be worse."

He gave me a withering look.

"Get me something I can read . . . anything on or by Rilke, Lowell, Baudelaire."

He paused, then added, "You want me to spell those for you?"

"Ronnie, lose the attitude, or you'll lose the fuckin' lip. Can *you* spell that?"

He picked up James Baldwin, asked, "What were his deathbed words?"

"Fuck should I know."

"Not that . . . he said 'I'm bored.' "

"I thought that was George Sanders."

"You thought wrong, he shot himself because he was bored. My namesake died of somewhat normal circumstances. However, your answers reveal a muddled tabloid intelligence. Suitable for donkey work."

I was leaving when he shouted, "Yo' . . . Gorilla, this music! Surely you jest . . . Whitney Houston."

He dropped the cassettes on the floor, continued, "I shall require some Elgar . . . Bach . . . or even Beethoven. But only as a last resort. How am I supposed to wash, pray tell?"

He was a spunky little fucker, I'll give him that . . . or he was nuts. I asked, "Your verbals reveal a bit too much mate. You're obviously a man of culture, of refined tastes. Am I correct?"

"One tries."

"No doubt you'll be familiar with a French whore's bath?"

"I beg your pardon?"

"What it is, I bring a basin of water and you use that."

"I most certainly will not."

"Ronnie . . . Ronnie, this is getting like a bad song. Then . . . you don't wash. As for toilet facilities, that complicated job at the foot of the cot is a chemical toilet . . . state of the art. Let me promise you one thing, however. You call me names again . . . any names, washing won't be a problem . . . Esso es claro."

Apart from his muttering "A kidnapping linguist" the message got through. At least for then.

Dex had gone but he'd left a note: "Some greedy-guts left us juiceless, the inhumanity of man."

No doubt he was already before his wardrobe selecting a persona. Clothes indeed make the man.

Breakfast for me was more coffee. No eggs. As I sipped, I glanced through a magazine Lisa had left on the table.

She'd red-marked lines from a feature on Kathy Galloway's "Love Burning Deep".

The poem, "Going Over" had many red lines. It looked like this:

You have burned your bridges
You have passed through the gate marked "no
return"

And for you there's no going back
No going back to the security of the known,
familiar house
to the well-known dispensations and the
threadbare coverings.

Now you are out there in unchartered territory
Heavy with threat and shadows not yet entered
The risks are high and yet you strike out boldly
guided only by unwavering conviction
And the longing for the true centre of the land
This is what it means to do a new thing

And yet you travel lightly
You are abandoned, given up in all things
to the task that lies ahead
You have inhabited yourself
You are home
And home is where you are even if it is a desert
No one can dispossess you of your own dwelling
This is what it means to be free.

Now, the very last few lines were under red ink gone riot,
as if the continuous re-emphasising would drive home
the message. Certainly drove it home to me.

We stand, one foot upon the bridge
Wondering if we too have the courage to go over
And strike the match behind us.

So rapt was I by the last line, I didn't hear her. She
snatched the magazine from me, clutched it to her bosom,

flared, "Ain't yo got no decency white boy, no sense of privacy?"

"Hey, back off . . . I didn't know it was sacred."

She rummaged in the fridge.

"Where de juice at?"

"Dex took it."

"Muthah-fuckhah."

To ease her down, I asked, "What will you do with the money?"

She mellowed. "Armistead Maupin's character, Anna Madrigal, said she'd like to buy a small Greek island . . . but on reflection, she settle for a small Greek."

I wondered if I had wandered into her "A" Level English class. This morning I had culture coming out of my arsehole.

Did I share this? Hell no. I told her of Dex's plans. He was going to open a pet cemetery. She didn't laugh, but asked, "Like Stephen King . . . is there a demand?"

"Well, there's already an existing one. At Silvermere in South-West London. Seems there's three horses buried there. I think, in fact, I used to back them. Oh yeah, they've got a goldfish, a family of rats, a terrapin, a monkey and a parrot. He showed me a price list for the deceased . . . and should I say pet-ceased?"

"It's what you'd expect from South-West London. Whole place is a fuckin' graveyard. How much to bury a dog?"

"About £500. But for your five big ones, you get a small burial service and a headstone. Course you could just cremate for £40."

She gave a small smile.

"Or better yet, leave it outside a Chinese restaurant."

We were almost close then. An intimacy tugged above

us and I felt such a wave of tenderness. She looked vulnerable when she laughed, as if the world hadn't yet attacked. The moment was lost as a loud crash came from the basement. She said, "Money can't be everything if God gave it to Madonna and Julio Iglesias."

Below, Baldwin had smashed the cot against the wall, but the chain held. As I approached him, he dropped to the ground and began a series of furious push-ups. I watched. He was a fit little bugger. After he ceased, he said, "You're a bouncer, right?"

Got me.

"Why do you say that?"

"Could be your scintillating conversation. Clubs are my business and you have the stance of a bouncer."

"Well, Ronnie, my man. Let me tell you something. If you want to keep breathing, keep your observations to yourself. There's no cookie for clever dicks, just a hole in the ground."

He gave me a studied look. What he saw, he didn't relish if his expression was any indicator.

"How very B-feature, dare one say. London Noir. Do you prepare these muscle replies in advance?"

"Ronnie . . . is this yer normal disposition? The constant arsehole. Christ, who's going to pay for your return? I mean, how keen could they possibly be for your company? What I'd like to know is how on earth you ever survived till now."

"Tell me," he said, "was my drink spiked last night . . . what?"

"You were bumped, animal tranquilliser."

"No irony meant, I'm sure . . . and the bump on my head . . . an actual animal?"

"My colleague, you don't want to meet him. Not a man of letters, alas."

"Where's my books?"

"Easy with that demanding tone, Ronnie, lest you want twin lumps. Anyway, who the fuck is Rilke?"

"One fears the *Duino Elegeies* would be somewhat lost on you . . . however

'Who, if I cried out, would ever hear me among
the angelic orders and
even if one of them took me suddenly to his heart,
I would lose identity
in his strange being.
For beauty's only the dawning of terror, we're
hardly able to bear and
adore
because it serenely disdains to destroy us.
Each angel is terrible.' "

Reciting this at the top of his voice.

I had to roar, "You wanna keep it down Ronnie—they'll hear you in Brixton."

"Close . . . are we?"

"Nice try Sherlock."

He bowed.

"I think even you'll agree these opening lines have a certain relevance."

"Well Ronnie, I think I'll leave you and Rilke to it."

"For solitude is really an inner matter," he boomed.

Turning up the stairs again, I felt something in my back pocket. The mask. I'd never put it on. I didn't think I'd share this with my chums. Ronnie was unlikely to tell.

*

As I came into the living room, my heart jumped sideways.

A completely bald man was sitting on the sofa.

"Whatcha think?' asked Dex. "Radical or wot?"

He ran a hand over his naked dome, smiled.

Radical was one way of terming it. The transformation was extraordinary. He now looked the total psycho ... which he was.

"There's more," he said.

He buried his head in his hands, there was a loud pss-ish and he had a full head of hair again. The bald cover he threw at me.

"Try it on Kojak."

I didn't catch it and let it fall at my feet. Whatever rubberised material was in it, it jerked and shuddered. For all the world, I thought, like my old dad's liver. I asked him, "Ever heard of Rilke?"

"One of the Baader Meinhof."

Lisa's voice cut off any reply I might have fronted.

"He was the poet of solitude. A constant traveller. He ended as a recluse in a château at Muzot. The *Duino Elegies* took him twelve years to complete. In his life he won a huge following of female admirers. *Sonnets to Orpheus* and *Elegies* are highly regarded."

She suddenly stopped. Dex said, "Bit of a ladies' man, was he, liked to roger the old fräuleins eh?"

I asked, "Jeez, how do you know this stuff?"

Dex answered, " 'Cos her old mum's a teacher."

Lisa glanced at me like a stranger, went into the kitchen. The sound of banging cups drew me after her. I said, "And hello to you, darlin'."

"Fuck off."

I grabbed her arm.

"Don't you ever dismiss me like that. I'm not some hired help. You want to throw a moody, I'll throw you out so fucking fast you won't touch ground. Am I getting through to you Lisa?"

She jumped at me, ground her hips into mine and her tongue deep in my mouth. Her hand unzipped me and a few seconds later she dropped to her knees.

"What about Dex?" I gasped.

"I ain't blowing him."

I told myself I didn't want to, my body screamed, "Oh yeah."

A few moments later it was over.

She stood, went to the sink, rinsed her mouth. She said, "You were saying . . ."

That evening, she was curled on the couch rolling a joint. I said, "Time to make the call."

"Not making any call."

"Lisa, you want this thing to go down? Come on, you've got to call her."

"Or wot Nico, you gonna beat on de woman? Oh lawdy, oh puleez mistah, don't go hitting on de woman."

God, I was tempted. Highly tempted. So I made the call. Baldwin's wife answered on the first ring. I said, "You've had a day. Are you going to pay?"

"Yes."

I told her the amount, the arrangements I'd give her tomorrow. To everything she replied simply "Yes". Nothing else, just a line of yesses. Then she put the phone down.

I roared, "She hung up."

Lisa said, "What, you were hoping for a date, that it?"

"Don't mouth me Lisa."

"I thought I did already. In the kitchen when you were making all those noises . . . uh . . . uh . . . oh . . . all . . . as if you were dying or somefink."

She emphasised the "fink" in a perfect parody of my accent.

I'd about had it with my "team".

"You're bored with our little enterprise, Lisa? The excitement palling already? That's fine with me. I'll just go down and cut our captive loose—'No hard feelings Mr Baldwin, we've changed our minds . . . sorry for the inconvenience.'—mebbe you could call a cab for him. Say the word, I'll do it. Try me."

She stretched, stubbed out the joint on the floor . . . *my* floor . . . gave an exaggerated yawn, said, "Oh, I don't think Dex would like that."

"Fuck Dex."

"I wonder if you'd be able."

Before I could hammer out a suitably macho reply, she said in a very quiet voice, "Did I ever tell you my angel story. I don't think anyone's heard it."

Baldwin's line from Rilke "Each angel is terrible" briefly flickered. I thought maybe the dope had kicked in and drawn her headlong on to mellowness. I was glad of anything that took the hard edge off. She continued, "When I was a little girl, the best thing to happen was to be selected as an angel for the school nativity play. Only white girls ever played Mary. Sounds like a title for a Mary Gordon novel, doesn't it?

"My dream came true, I was to be an angel. The day before the play I heard the principal say to the drama teacher, 'You can't have a nigger angel, there aren't any jungle bunnies in heaven.'

"They took away my halo. For a long time I was a sad little girl 'cos they had no rabbits in heaven. Later, of course, I learnt that they didn't mean rabbits, not the cuddly type anyway."

She looked up at me and smiled.

"So you see, Nicky, mon cherie, I don't want to be a fuckin' angel . . . OK?"

The toilet facilities for our guest were basic. That chemical job had cost me a fair bit though. Thing was, I got to lug it back and forth. Dex reckoned the humiliation alone should keep Baldwin docile. As I got to do the ferrying, I think the process somewhat backfired.

As I did this now, Baldwin smirked. I said, "Keep it up buddy, I'll stick yer friggin' head in it . . . tell you, Baldwin, if I might apply a little toilet metaphor here, you're a royal pain in the arse."

He laughed, said, "To quote Anthony Burgess, 'The Royal Family do not help, they are philistines, they like horses.' Your colleague paid me a visit. Showed me his cannon."

"What?"

"Oh yes, he explained to me it was a Ruger Blackhawk .44 Magnum. He wished me to suck it . . . the gun that is. At least I think it was . . . one lives in quiet hope."

"Jesus."

"No damage done, it was a replica I understand. Not that it was any less dramatic. More worrying perhaps that a grown man buys toy guns. Is he the leader?"

I had no comment. I finished slopping out . . . badly. Baldwin roared, "Some Rilke I think:

'My occupation, soon it will be my vocation, is to
have patience;
sometimes it is as with a pain
that one thinks one cannot
possibly endure a moment longer
and yet it slowly becomes part
of one's everyday life
—human nature is tough.' "

I asked, "You think old Rilke would have done this
poetically? Believe me . . . there is no poetry in shit."

He seemed delighted, replied, "The barbarian thinks,
how illuminating. A quote worthy of the TLS. How suc-
cinctly put."

I took a step towards him.

"I warned you about the name-calling Mr Baldwin."

"You needn't call me Mister. You don't work for me . . .
at least not yet."

And so he ranted, I didn't know if it was the Rilke
wanker or himself. Shite anyway. Here he was: "The fear
that I could betray myself and say all the things I am
afraid of, and the fear that I could not say anything at
all because it is all unsayable."

I didn't analyse why I paid attention to that piece.

Threats only seemed to encourage him and I was weary
hitting him so I said, "It's goodnight fella. Anything you
want as this is it till morning?"

"My cup overfloweth, I rest content . . . oh, by the way,
whose is the woman . . . yours or Clint Eastwood's?"

"What woman?"

"Don't insult my nose . . . I smell 'Poison'."

"You're a perfume connoisseur as well . . . is that it?"

"I ought to know that brand. It's my kiss-off to . . . how shall I term them . . . my cast-offs . . ."

"You're sure your missus is going to want you back. What does she use?"

"Her rather splendid mind."

I flicked off the light. The bizarre thing is I think he was content. As I reached the top of the stairs he whispered, "Hey Attila . . . shut the door."

Lisa was gone. To change her clothes or something, her attitude preferably. I rang Bonny, arranged to meet her at the Crown. Anything to get out of the flaming house. I felt I'd been kidnapped. In many ways I had.

I went upstairs to check Lisa's cosmetics. Sitting among them, a bottle of Poison. I'd unscrewed the top and was sniffin' it when for some reason I glanced at the window. A panda car . . . then the knock at the door . . . I bolted down, my heart fucked.

Two uniforms.

"Good evening, Sir, might we step in a moment."

"What's the problem?"

"Really Sir, best if we came inside."

In they came.

"We've had a complaint about noise."

"Just a few friends around. Won't happen again."

"You the owner, Sir?"

"Yes . . . I . . ."

One of the uniforms looked towards the basement . . .

"That lead somewhere, Sir?"

Before I could reply, if I could, the other let out a cry, "Merle Haggard . . . you a Country fan?"

He threw an appreciative eye over my collection. I said, "Feel free to borrow whatever you fancy."

He selected an armful.

"If I might just . . ."

"Of course."

Then he said to the other, "No need to trouble this gentleman further George . . . is there. Country music has got to be loud."

As they got to the door, he too looked at the basement.

"Bit of a hooten-Annie down there . . . the old square dancing."

"Something like that . . . yes."

"Mebbe I'll drop round, cut the rug with you. I don't advise you to drink that, it's poison . . ."

I looked down, in my left hand was Lisa's open perfume bottle, the name clearly legible. I said in a weak voice, "Next time I'll have Lone Star . . . OK?"

I shut the door, my knees went, I slid to the floor.

A while later, Dex came banging and I let him in.

"Jeez Nick, what happened to you, you're pale as Michael Jackson."

"The old Bill were here."

"Yes, I know. I called them."

"What?"

"Dual purpose really. Throw them off the scent and sharpen up our act here. We're getting sloppy . . . need to get lean and mean. How'd it go, get the old juices flowing . . . give you back yer edge?"

I couldn't answer.

I went to the fridge. Bingo, there was a can of Coca-Cola. Back to the living room, I front lobbed it and shouted, "Catch."

He near fell over, but he got it. Before he could right himself, I kicked his legs from under him and planted a foot on his chest. I opened the Coke, it exploded from the can and I poured it into his face.

"Tell me Dex . . . does it taste like the real thing?"

"What?"

"Not a replicant, is it?"

"Ah . . ."

"Where is it?"

"I sold it to a drunk paddy."

I bounced the can off his forehead.

"Go away," I said, "before I get very fucking mean."

My hands shook as I dressed but I realised I hadn't done any dope all day. Behaved like one, sure. I felt the vague promise of a treacherous hope.

The pub was humming. Bonny was at the counter. A middle-aged guy was pulling chat on her. No wonder as she as wearing

a short black dress

black tights

black patent heels, killer high

the whole

"hey-wanna-fuck-me-stupid-fellah"

outfit.

"Nick . . . this is . . . sorry, what did you say your name is?"

"Brian."

He was dressed in the ultra-faded denim. One more wash and it's gone. The look caught between haute couture and oval panhandler. A delicate balance. His smile and hair colour accessorised exactly. And King's Road workboots, the kind that yell he never did a day's work in his life.

A sour look flashed at me. I smiled. The evening had promise. Bonny had ordered large Scotches, beer chasers, raised her glass.

"Tiddley pip."

"That too," I said.

Brian was something in electronics, or was that the other way round. Who gave a rat's arse?

He was desperate to suss out our relationship and figured he was already halfway to first base with Bonny.

. . . figured wrong.

He was chewing nuts. Bonny said, "You want a definition of hell?"

"Sure."

"Englishmen in shorts."

Brian turned quickly to me.

"And your field is?"

"Thuggery."

"Excuse me?"

"I'm a thug. I beat up people . . . for money. But sometimes I just do it for the hell of it . . . you know how it is Bri, when you love your work, you just can't leave it alone."

All the time I was smiling. Good ole boy version, like Merle Haggard on the album cover. Felt good too. The thought skittled across my mind that I was more like Dex than I wanted to admit.

Brian turned to Bonny. "He's pulling my leg . . . isn't he Bon?"

She gave him her most sincere look.

"No . . . that's what he does. But tonight is his night

off. Isn't it darlin' . . . or was that yesterday . . . oh and Bri, don't call me Bon . . . OK?"

Her lipstick had snagged on her top tooth. Nothing makes a woman look more vulnerable than that. I could have loved her then.

"Well," I said, "tonight I don't expect to be paid . . . but who's counting . . . eh?"

Brian suddenly remembered the car parked on the old double yellow and had to rush. Most used getaway line in the business but effective.

"Hurry back," I said.

Bonny rested her hand on my knee.

"You're in mighty form."

"And the night is young, let's get some serious Scotch flowing. Yo', bar-keep!"

Rilke never crossed my mind.

Bonny said, "See when you lighten up, you're almost a fun guy."

"Not so dark eh . . . less black in fact. Thing is Bonny, you're a woman and an attractive one. If you live to be a hundred, you'll never know what it's like not to be a good-looking guy. Fun ain't it. I placed an ad in those personal columns once. The end result was I was to meet this woman outside Burger King in Leicester Square. She never showed up. But I think she did, had a look from a safe distance and then fucked off. I pinned her letter to the glass, all her details. Who knows, mebbe she got lucky."

Later we hit a new club in the West End called the Deep South. They play some mean low-down Cajun and play it live. A fiddle player, he was bewitched in his artistry. Dance to that the devil said. We did and for as long as they dished it out.

All the while I was hammerin' down these boiler makers. I can't dance . . . need I say more about the state I was in. With a woman who made me feel I *could* dance. That's the rarest kind. The awful thing is . . . you get the knowledge after you let 'em go and you're not ever going to dance again.

Not like that anyway.

She looks at you with shining eyes and you're the guy you always wanted to be. You feel almost tanned! Then, you get to thinking, she's just the music, the accompaniment . . . not the creator. The magic's gone. Once . . . mebbe once, you get that lucky and let it skip away. The first time it's a free gift . . . ever after, you have to earn it . . . and it isn't ever worth it. Elvis has left the building and you weren't looking.

There's a huge Boots in Piccadilly Circus. With plate-glass windows. Before going to the club, I stood at the end of the window and raised my arm and leg. Bonny was treated to the optical illusion of me with multi limbs. Harry Worth used to open his show with this. Back when I was a kid.

"Who's Harry fucking Worth?" the kids ask.

My old man would have been in their corner. As soon as the show began, he'd roar, "Not that four-eyed wanker."

Which, if you were to take his words literally, would indeed have been some optician effect. I think old Harry was held in such affection by others, as he reflected a safe cosy England when Morris Minors ruled the road. The only drugs were aspirin and smoking was a social requirement.

No one had learnt of calories, carbohydrates, polyunsaturates or ozone. You could eat what you liked. Dex said they called anorexia poverty then. Harry was a hybrid of Frank Spencer and yer dotty uncle. The Krays loved their old mum and there was no breakfast TV.

Bonny and I ate tacos under Eros and I told her the rules of behaviour as outlined by James Crumley.

He says there are rules of conduct in America that can change your luck in a country based on the rules of luck. After forty, never go any place you've never been before. Except on somebody else's cash. Never go out at night unless you're wearing black. And never go anywhere without a gun.

I dunno where we'd got the thunderbird but it was washing down the food a treat. Also, alas, seriously affecting my judgement. I took Bonny back to the house in Clapham.

I surfaced around eight the next morning. A manic thirst chanting
> Water
> Water
> Water

I got out of bed quickly and wow was that ever a mistake. A roaring headache nigh split me and the sickness in my stomach was biblical. A hazy series of memories bounced around. The remembrance of tacos past drove me to my knees. Then I looked for Bonny. Her black dress was crumpled at the end of the bed, plus my clothes. Twisted round each other like a weak petition.

In the bathroom, I spewed up a few times, checked my face in the mirror. God-on-a-tandem, it looked like something died a horrible death. Dragged myself downstairs. Bonny was sitting at the kitchen table, in one of my old shirts. Dex was seated opposite, his arms folded. Seeing me he said, "The dead arose and appeared to . . . two. What news from Jerusalem?"

I put my hand on Bonny's head, asked, "Alright honey?"

She didn't answer. Dex answered benignly . . .

"What's going on?" I asked.

Dex said, "I thought I'd look in on our guest early. Make sure he hadn't croaked. See if he'd specific newspaper preference. Have him down as the *Daily Telegraph* type. Know what I mean, he leaks notions. But I digress. Bejapered Seamus, who do I meet coming up the stairs . . . but the bold Bonny. She looked at me as if I were Fred West or something."

He waited for my comment. I had none so he continued, "Well Nico old pal, you could have blown me down with the proverbial feather. Did somebody . . . somehow neglect to tell the Dexter we'd a new player. So what I thought we'd do, Bonny and I, was wait quietly here. Grab a little quality time and then see what Nick would suggest."

I laid my hand on Bonny's shoulder, said, "Go upstairs, get dressed."

She looked to Dex who said, "Thank you for attending the interview. Naturally I can't tell if you've been successful as there are others for me to see. However, I do like the cut of your jib, by jove I do. Send in the next applicant."

He waved his hand in a gesture of busy dismissal.

I eased myself into her chair.

"So what have we got Dex?"

"What we've got is a problem."

"She won't talk."

"Tut-tut Nicky, lesson one. All women talk, it's their nature."

"You're going to have to trust me on this one."

A wave of nausea walloped me. I got shakily to my feet and went to the front room. I located some brandy and, with shaking hands, took a hefty belt. Like petrol with a vicious side. It hit my stomach hard, hard as truth. But stayed. Dex had naturally followed, he said, "Nice going, Nick. Bad sign is the old morning pick-me-up. Hair of the dog I guess. Thing is, you'll want the whole animal before noon. Maybe later, you could introduce Baldwin to the rest of the neighbourhood. Let's see, we could have a car boot sale instead of the ransom."

I began to feel better. Artificial sure, but didn't care where the recovery came from. You couldn't say things were so much slipping away from me as in a full gallop. I tried to focus, said, "What had you in mind?"

"You won't like it."

"Jeez, wouldn't that be a novelty . . . What?"

"Whack her."

"Whack her . . . like terminate with extreme prejudice. What kind of a movie do you think this is? An English version of *Wise Guys* . . . and you're who . . . Joe Pesci?"

He gave a disappointed shrug.

"Aw, I kinda saw myself in the De Niro role . . . but OK . . . Joe Pesci is good."

I stood up, steadier . . . getting there.

"Go home Dex, leave this to me."

"No can do ole buddy-mio. The Dexter's got roots."

He sauntered into the kitchen and began to set the breakfast table, shouted, "Settings for three I presume?"

The brandy kicked in and I landed in the twilight zone between health and death. It's like living behind glass or I guess what the Catholics call Purgatory. They usually have a word for pain.

I went upstairs. Bonny was dressed, the black outfit looked sad. Is there owt as pathetic as last night's glad rags, like a disco in the morning light. I pulled out a raincoat, said, "An old raincoat will never let you down."

"What?"

"Rod Stewart! Don't worry love, you're going home. I'll call you a cab ... no, no ... don't say anything. I'll call you tonight."

I was rummaging in the cupboard when she whispered, "How could you?"

No reply to that, then or now. I found my old black hold-all and tested it's weight. Yeah, holding heavy. Back downstairs I rang a cab and heard the toast pop. I would see Dex flip the toast like a pizza. He was whistling ... sounded like "Fernando."

I brought the bag into the kitchen, asked, "Are you familiar with Ecclesiastics: 'A man's dress tells you what he does ... and: A man's work tells you what he is.' "

Dex, unsure of where this was going, quipped, "Intimately ... words to live by."

But always a game participant, he added, "Shoot the men in suits."

I unzipped the bag and he ventured, "A run before brekkie. How wise, help distil the quart of brandy you had. They'll smell you coming, eh?"

God, I was glad he was enjoying it.

"Dex, you know what I work at, hell, you even know *where* I used to work. But you've never actually *seen* me work. Let's remedy that right now."

I pulled out a baseball bat.

"This beauty here is the Louisville slugger and if you listen carefully, you'll hear a whoosh."

I put everything behind my swing, all the brandied ferocity and swept the breakfast things across the kitchen.

"Did you hear it, did you catch the whoosh . . . no, pay attention, you can't miss it."

He'd backed up against the wall . . .

I took another swing and crushed the toaster.

"I think you heard it that time. Breakfast is cancelled . . . OK? Now let's all stop fucking around. We'll collect the money and that's an end to it . . . esso es claro."

He nodded.

When the cab came, I paid him in advance. Bonny never spoke, just staring dead-eyed ahead. Not that I expected gratitude for covering the tab. I was still operating on her money as it was. Dex took off soon after and he hadn't a whole lot of repartee either.

Back inside I lay on the sofa and wondered what had become of Harry Worth.

S.O.S. claro . . . my old man used to shout. Esso es claro.
Is it clear?

"Yeah, loud and fuckin'."

He'd been a merchant seaman and that was the sole
thing he'd learnt. Not about drinkin', he'd picked that up
before he left. I smile to think he finally got to school, a
drinking one. They're a movable feast but mainly the
school has a West End location. Sometimes he's leader of
the pack, other times he *is* the pack. The very last time
I saw him he was shouting that he'd never stop drinking
until the last hostage was free. But just in case, he added
a rider, "Or as long as there's even a hint of a hostage
being taken."

Dex came by a few hours later with a lemon, a bottle
of tequila, a pack of Marlboro.

"Peace offering," he said.

"Why not?"

"I was going to bring bagels and styrofoams of coffee . . .
have us an American time, especially as you tend to be
armed and dangerous in the kitchen. No need to go in
there again."

He had a Brooklyn accent to match.

"So why the tequila?"

"I thought fuck Plan A for a game of soldiers, let's get
loaded."

At long last I could slip in a wee anecdote. I said, "John Wayne said that tequila hurt his back."

"His back!"

"Yeah, every time he drank it, he fell off the stool."

He didn't seem too impressed. But fuck, I'd been sitting on it for years. How often does the chance to slide that into a conversation occur?

We sucked the lemons, knocked back the tequila and even had the hit of salt. We were almost cordial. Dex even had a worn zippo to complement the Marlboro. He said, "I went to see Alex la Igliesia's debut, *Acción Mutante*."

I couldn't fix a connection so said unsteadily, "He's a Mexican?"

"Never heard of him, did you? Not a name bandied around much in the Clint Eastwood fan club. Even you'll have heard of the Spanish film maker Pedro Almodóvar."

I hadn't.

"Christ, just how thick are you . . . only kidding buddy. Have some more tequila. Well Almodóvar financed this pic as he believed in it . . . now the raison d'être for this cinematic excursion. There's a spoof TV bulletin in it about a kidnapping. The ransom demand appears like figures on a scoreboard."

"You're thinking of the ransom?"

"Flunked out again Nick. I was thinking about lezzies."

"Lassies?"

"What . . . now you're hard of hearing . . . lemme spell it out for you . . . l-e-s-b-i-a-n-s. Last night I read Ann Bannon's *I'm a Woman*."

I couldn't fly with his rapid-fire-changes of topic. Mostly I wanted to ask him why but I was afraid he'd tell me. I said nothing and he began to quote from the story:

"I know most of the girls in here, I've probably slept with half of them. I've lived with half of the half I've slept with.

"I've loved half of the half I've slept with."

He waited for my response.

"You lost me at the very first half."

It was like he hadn't heard me, either way . . . he could care less.

"The best bit, Nicky, this chick who's talking . . . she turns to her mate and says, 'What does it all come to? You know something baby? It doesn't matter. Nothing matters. You don't like me and that doesn't matter. Some-day maybe you'll love me and that *won't* matter either.' "

I noticed he was wearing cowboy boots. They were stiff in newness. Welcome to Marlboro country. He lit a ciga-rette, the only sound being the heavy clunk as he shut down the zippo.

"So Nico, you're a bit of a cowboy . . . yeah, give me yer Western verdict."

"Well, Dex, there's a point to all of it."

"Naturellement, you heard the end line."

"Run it by me again."

"Nothing matters . . . not a cussed thing . . . that way you can't lose. It's all just a Spanish movie . . . not main-stream."

"Yeah," I said.

After he'd left, the tequila in my system called out for music. I no longer had Hank Williams as the cop had "borrowed" those. I thought he had taste as well as cheek.

Lisa has said to me, "Doesn't cost anything to be gentle now and then. It's not a weakness."

Oh yeah.

"Look Lisa, I don't know any gentle types. It's not a quality there's much percentage in. Gentle people cost."

She gave a mild sneer.

"Cost . . . the white man's price on everything."

"Hey, you think I'm kidding here Lisa. You get to know these people, you get to like them but they're casualties. No matter how you watch for them, they go down. One way or another. Then you hurt. No, stay clear."

She'd begun to roll a joint and then took a small phial from her bag.

"Seasoning?" I asked.

"Liquid demorol, they give it to cancer patients."

"And you flavour your dope with it . . . very fucking gentle."

The booze had mellowed me and I cleared the debris from the kitchen. Fixed some food for the guest. He was in a yoga position, the picture of tranquillity. He said, "Do I remind you of the panther?"

"What, 'cos you're black?"

"Rilke's panther . . . listen . . . can you hear him . . . see

'As he paces in cramped circles
over and over, the monument of
his powerful soft strides
is like a ritual dance
around a centre in which
a mighty will
stands paralysed.' "

"Give it a rest, eh."

He considered, then nodded his head, said, "I made Bonny's acquaintance."

"I heard."

"Her age is indeterminable. I'll kindly venture forty. Martin Amis tells us that by that age, we have the face we deserve."

"He'd know. I told her I didn't think she looked that. She said it's what forty looks like nowadays."

"There is a fact of nature I'm going to share with you."

"Don't bother."

"I must insist. It is possible to sneak up on a fox. But a vixen, never. No matter what direction you come from, she'll always have her eyes on you."

He was well pleased with this little nomily. I asked, "What am I to make of that?"

"Perhaps that he who hunts with the hounds might yet run with the hare."

"You want this food or not, age isn't improving it."

"What culinary delight have you devised to whet my gastronomic juices?"

"That means 'Wot's to eat?'... Right? It's yer favourite... eggs. No toast due to an industrial accident."

Then I left him to it. I rang his wife and read her the Riot Act. "Don't contact the police... Type of bills, denominations... Be ready in twenty-four hours for the drop."

Kidnapping kind of stuff.

To all she replied "Yes."

I figured she was a) in deep shock b) on drugs c) couldn't care less.

Only a) could be in our interest.

I heard shouting from the basement... I didn't go down, just roared.

"What, what is it now?"

He bellowed, " 'Only at times/the curtain of the pupil lifts/—quietly.'

"That's the part of the poem you should remember my bouncing Lothario."

I thought he'd finished but no.

"One more thing."

"Jesus, wot?"

"You might try to remember one little item."

"Oh yeah, and what might that be?"

"The mask, try and wear it the odd time, just for the appearance of the thing . . . OK."

I didn't even know where it was any more or for that matter, the position of anything else either. I went back to bed, I wanted to go back to the brandy but some sanity ruled. The phone jerked me awake. Late evening.

Bonny.

In a cold voice she said, "I'm going to leave London in a few days. Perhaps on my return I'll read about you in the papers."

I struggled to wake.

"Lisa . . . Lisa . . . oh shit . . . sorry, I'm half asleep Bonny . . . I meant Bonny, it's that I'm still groggy here."

There was a sharp intake of breath from her. I felt it like a razor then.

"That says it all."

"Don't worry about Dex . . . I'll make sure he stays away."

"It's not Dex I'm afraid of."

Then she hung up.

I told myself, "This is good . . . she's safer away . . . till I get things sorted . . . it's good . . . definitely I'm well pleased . . . things couldn't be better."

I was wrong.

Bonny was wrong.

All dreadfully so.

I went downstairs. Dex and Lisa were rolling a joint. I said, "We do it tomorrow."

Dex answered, "Oh yippee, I've got my little bag with 'swag' printed on it all prepared."

"The plan is the same, no variation. Now get the fuck out of my house."

The remainder of the evening is lost to me. I guess I fed Baldwin, and no doubt he fed me the usual poetic bullshit. It's a given that I fed my neuroses. Fighting the urge to get drunk all over again. A quiet voice promising if I started, I might never stop. I wasn't sure I'd want to.

Was it torment?

Dex had said you couldn't truly understand torture till you heard William Shatner's version of "Lucy in the Sky with Diamonds."

Maybe I hummed a few bars.

Next morning I asked Baldwin if his wife would pay.

"She'll pay."

"You're very sure."

"It's my business . . . certainty."

"I dunno Baldwin, she doesn't say a whole lot. I gave her instructions, to have old unmarked bills. No consecutive serial numbers. All the usual stuff. She only ever says 'yes' . . . nowt else . . . just that friggin' 'yes'."

"She doesn't talk to garbage. It's why I married her."

This said without even bothering to look at me. A tap on the head might have got his attention but I wasn't up to it. As I turned to go he said, "Goliath . . . ponder this as an epilogue, if not a conclusion. My Rilke was fascinated with contained energy. Ah, if I had but the time or inclination to recite. 'The Gazelle', or 'The Flamingos'.

"Living creatures confined by restriction."

He shook the leg chain and gave a grim smile. One that never touched his eyes.

"There is much I should like to say, but as time goes by, I become more distrustful of myself—monster that I am, having never been so deeply, painfully and unceasingly concerned about any creature as about myself."

I didn't reply. The word was so crucial to him.

Lisa and Dex arrived early. We ran through the plan again. She was wearing a formal black two-piece suit and looked like a highly successful businesswoman.

Or, a dominatrix.

Dex and I wore sports jackets, slacks, open shirts. A Marks and Spencer's mildly comfortable look. Not rich, but not hurtin'.

At noon, I made the call.

"Mrs Baldwin, you have the money?"

"Yes."

"OK, it's 12 now. At 1.30, you are to enter Marks and Spencer's flagship shop at Marble Arch. You'll have the money in one of their bags. Go to a changing room in the women's department. Leave the money on the floor there. Walk out of the store and then right. Keep walking for exactly five minutes. Then you'll be contacted. Any questions?"

A flood: "When do I get my husband back? How can I be sure he's alright—have you hurt him?"

I considered my reply carefully and then I said "Yes".

And hung up.

I turned to my merry band, said, "OK pranksters, let's hit the bricks."

*

At 1.30, Lisa and I had already purchased a dressing gown. It rested in the large bag. We were standing near to the escalator. Lisa moved suddenly.

"That's her in the blonde hair, cheap leather coat."

"Go," I said and nodded to Dex.

The place was crowded as we'd anticipated. Lisa took a dress from the rail. Mrs Baldwin had selected a cardigan and she was carrying the distinctive green bag. They disappeared into the changing rooms. A few moments lapsed and Mrs Baldwin emerged carrying only the cardigan. Then Lisa, with her green bag, took the escalator to furnishings.

I went after her.

Dex was on the ground floor to follow Mrs Baldwin. We were on the street and going left in under five minutes. The green bag was now in a Selfridges hold-all.

At Bond Street tube station, I said to Lisa, "I'll hang on to the money . . . then tonight . . . if it's all clear . . . I'll meet you at my place. About 7, like that."

She gave me a long look, said, "You wouldn't skip on us now, would you precious?"

"And leave me home in Clapham . . . an Englishman's castle and all that shit."

She touched my cheek with one finger.

"Now all dis near over baby, we go back to sweet loving like before."

"I can hardly contain myself."

"You all hurry home now. I be keeping it warm for mah daddy."

I watched her go. I walked out of the station, hailed a cab.

I had the driver swing by Bonny's cafe. What did I think . . . I'd see her at work . . . and then what? Shovel out a few wedges of cash . . . what?

I saw smoke from the top of Clapham Rise. Before I could think, the cabby said, "Torched the cafe last night. Had to bring in the fire engines from Streatham to fight the blaze. The owner was trapped in it."

I choked down hard and as we actually passed, I locked my feet and tried to keep my eyes down. I could smell the smoke. I'll fuckin' always smell the smoke.

When we got to my street, I paid the cab, watched him drive off. Then I crossed to Dex's house . . . broke a back window and climbed in. Went to the front window and dropped the money at my feet. Said aloud, "Now let's see who shows up."

Lisa showed within twenty minutes. A light skip in her walk.

"Looking good," I thought.

Then ten minutes later, Dex. He stopped outside. A long look towards his house. I whispered, "Come on, come on in you twisted fuck."

But he didn't. Turned into my home. "Home is where the treachery is." As I figured on giving them a little time, I had a wander through Dex's home. Hotel rooms have more energy. It was: 1. Neat. 2. Antiseptic. 3. Vacant.

Anyone could have lived there or no one. I found a

bottle of gin and poured some into a mug. This had a cat's head on the side, underneath was the logo, "I love pussy."

"Cute," I said.

I had vaguely expected to find the browning automatic. Since it disappeared from under my fridge, I expected Dex had it. As was my quota now, I was absolutely wrong.

I checked the money, well I looked at it. Was it all there . . . probably. I counted a wad at random and it came to ten grand. These were an awful lot of wads. The money was old, near crumpled. I shouted aloud.

"I'm third of a millionaire. Wouldn't my old dad be surprised."

Hefting a thick wad, I lash-kicked it across the room. It hit the wall with a light thud and slithered to the floor. I said, "See Bonny, kicked a little your way . . . OK darling . . . OK sweetheart . . ."

A thought pondered into my head. This morning when I'd been running through my plan, Dex had been whistling quietly. One of those annoying things, you know you know it, but you're fucked if you can put a name to it. As we'd left the house he'd given me a look of what I could now only identify as triumph.

Now I could name it. Elton John's "Burn Down the Mission".

And I was relieved I hadn't found the gun. Oh yeah, I wanted to take him with my bare hands.

An hour passed. I left that money and went across the road. What I felt was "ready." The house was quiet. I headed for the basement and heard low moans.

"Christ," I thought, "they're torturing the poor bastard."

I'd waited too long.

Lisa was on her knees, giving Baldwin a blow job. His face had that rictus of torment that is total pleasure. His eyes looked on mine. I noticed for the first time his eyes were brown. Wouldn't Lisa be proud, I'd caught up. He shoved Lisa back.

"What," she said. "You didn't come."

She followed his look and her face twisted.

"Oh Nico . . . Nico . . . you weren't meant to come."

I said, "Someone's got to come."

Baldwin's leg was still chained. Heat of passion I guess. No sign of Dex.

Baldwin said, "Believe it or not old chummy, I finished with this bitch six years ago. But she hasn't given up . . . as you've just seen."

I looked at her, said, "All this to get him back . . . jeez Lisa . . . no wonder you knew Rilke so well. Who'd have thought you could care so much . . . you poor pathetic cow."

She put her hand out towards him.

"He's mine, he belongs to me."

And Baldwin laughed.

Lisa backed away. I swear she was whimpering. God, is there a more devastating sound in the whole world.

Baldwin said to me, "Oscar Wilde, I don't think I covered him in our lectures. Well, old Oscar said, you'll appreciate this: 'A woman will do anything for the man she loves.'"

And paused here for full effect.

"'*Except* stop loving him.'"

If he expected a reply, I didn't have one. He gave an

irritated shrug, said, "I haven't seen the bitch for six years, already she's on her knees."

Lisa was walking rapidly towards him, I saw the automatic as she said, "Here's six, you bastard."

And put that number of shots into him. His body jerked all over the cot but was held in place by the chain. Then he was still.

She turned to me. Tears streaming down her face. I started towards her and she whispered, "I'm so sorry Nick . . . you weren't the worst . . . just red-neck dumb."

And she squeezed the trigger:

> click
>
> click
>
> click

I said "It jams after six."

And swung my right fist with all the power I had, added, "What . . . I could have been a contender!"

It caught her up under the chin and I thought I heard her neck break. She fell back on Baldwin. I moved over to her and she was murmuring, "No more ange . . ."

"Rabbits maybe," I said, as gentle as I was able.

I found Dex in the kitchen. With his throat cut. A coffee cup still gripped in his hand. I turned him over to see if his face might tell me something. It told me nothing. At least nothing I wanted to hear. It took me a few moments but eventually my saliva returned and I spat full in his face.

Back at his house I found I hadn't quite finished my gin. I moved to an armchair and put the money under my feet. Then I moved a bit and rested them on it.

Better.

I sat wondering how difficult it would be to find a

Morris Minor. Tax and insurance, probably be sky high for an old car. One thing was certain, the colour: black.

They say you hear a sound in a person's throat as they die. A death rattle. I didn't hear Lisa's, not then. But now, I hear it all the time. And keep looking round, trying to locate it. Fuck, I know what it is . . . I just don't know where it's coming from. I remember a thing Dex told me during our tequila session. It seemed particularly fitting now. He'd sat up till the early morning, glued to the television at the beginning of the Gulf War. As the ferocious bombardment of Baghdad began, he'd shouted, "Fuck 'em if they can't take a joke."

PART THREE

I stayed sitting, sipping the gin. Not sure what I thought. Eventually they'd come and I'd face:

Four murders.

Arson.

Kidnapping.

Criminal trespass.

Burglary.

As I was the only one left, they'd throw the whole shit and kaboodle at me. I'd be a mini-serial sensation. My photo in the *Sun* and caption, "Bring Back Hanging". In prison the brothers would hurt me for offing two of theirs. The money would go back and I'd be full fucked.

OR

The whisper came about evening time . . .

"Dade County

      Big Apple

          Nashville

              Colorado

      Beeboopaloopbopwop."

A litany of hope.

And I thought, "Why the hell not." Go for it, I certainly had the cash . . . did I have the balls. Take the show on the road. If I'd come from the madness then I could certainly head for the final insanity . . . New York.

I got up and gathered the money. It was light for such

an amount. Crossed the street and back into the killing
zone. I stayed away from the kitchen and basement.
Upstairs, I showered and packed one small case. Lisa and
I had passports for our journey. Well, she wouldn't be
needing hers. I tossed it on the bed. The bottom drawer
had various drugs and I left them. Enough mind alter-
ation. It crossed my mind to go get the browning
automatic

. . . and see Lisa.

Fuck—no. I was looking for the land of the Saturday-
night special. Weapons were as common as burgers. I
threw the duffel bag of money on my shoulder and walked
out. I didn't look back. When all this unravelled, they'd
be hunting me with everything. Right now, I still had
time. Made my getaway on the tube and checked into a
small hotel in Notting Hill Gate. The owner was Indian
and greedy. When I heard the price I said, "Jeez, bit steep
is it mate, I'm not a tourist."

"Ah, I hope to bring my family over from the village."

"If I stay a few nights, you'll be able to bring over the
whole flaming village."

The room was instant depression. I pushed the money
under the bed and went out. He asked. "The room is to
your liking, Mister?"

"Pure heaven. I may never leave it."

Walked down Bayswater and everything was open.
First off, I bought some body belts, they're used to Arabs
there and these belts would hold a lot of cash. Which I
had. Next I bought a Sony walkman and then to select
some tapes. A huge promotion for a Scottish rock outfit
called "Gun". I had to have that. Especially as the album
was called, "Swagger".

For Dex.

Then I loaded up on Lorenna McKennet and Iris de Ment. A bookshop next and I couldn't find what I wanted. The assistant was in her twenties. A cross between a student and a wino. The arrogance was all her own and she clocked me as I approached.

But I could play. I'd had expert tuition. Start low.

"Excuse me, *Ms*."

Without a breath she said, "Thrillers are next to the horror section, on your left."

She didn't add, "You moron," but we both saw it hang there.

I said, "I was looking for something on Rilke."

"You mean Roethke . . . or possibly Rimbaud."

I caught her arm.

"Hey, I've had a day you wouldn't believe, OK, now trust me on this. I know Rilke like you'll never know fuckin' manners. So, what y'say, want us to go look?"

We did and found. I bought two volumes. Then the off-licence and a bottle of bourbon. If that's what they drank . . .

I turned into Paulbridge Gardens to open the tapes. Christ, they seal those cassettes like aspirations, light and useless. I'd got one out when a voice said, "Wotcher got there?"

I turned, two white youths dressed like blacks. That made me tired and sad. One glanced over his shoulder then back to me, said, "This is a hypodermic needle. Give us yer money fooker or you get AIDS."

In his hand, I saw the syringe. There was a term for those white boys who wanted to be black.

"Whiggers." That is, white niggers.

I thought arsehole did as well.

I said, "Are you familiar with Rainer Maria Rilke? Impressive first names, eh, I only just discovered them . . . here, catch."

And he put his hand up to block. I smashed my fist in his face. Heard the nose go. The other made to run and I grabbed him by his ponytail. Swung him into the wall, said, "There you go."

Bent and picked up the needle, hunkered beside the first.

"Old Rainer Maria used to talk about Quiet Lights. He said the big flashes come without warning and that a single experience of them should effect a full transformation of one's entire life."

He was groaning, trying to staunch the blood from his nose. I held the syringe up to the light, muttered, "AIDS . . . huh?"

And plunged it into his neck. Then I moved over to the other and rammed it in his arse. I picked up Rilke and began to walk away. A middle-aged woman was standing . . . transfixed. I said, "Not poetry lovers, but they're safe now, they've had their shots."

I brought my belongings back to the hotel. The money was still there. It crossed my mind to go and buy the place. I felt the owner would understand cash, he didn't seem the cheque type. Mainly what I felt was like the old story of the drunk. He knows he dropped his key in the dark alley, but he searches under the street light 'cos there's brightness there. Baldwin had said to me, "You're like a blind man in a dark room searching for a black cat that isn't there."

I'd intellectually rallied with, "Bollocks."

"Close, but we call it metaphysics."

One minute I'd be numb from horror . . . from grief, loss, betrayal. Next, I'd be zooming on my plans for America. What I was . . . was fucked and part-ways knew it. A drink would help so I tore the seal from the bourbon, chugged it from the bottle. And burn like a bastard it did. More . . . burn further.

In a little while, I was lit and put the earphones on. "Gun" nearly deafened me and I wrenched it out. Not enough bourbon for that racket. Then Iris de Ment . . . better. Ball-breaking sad, but bearable, drank on.

I'd seen the billboards across town, "Fly Virgin Atlantic". Would I get a pair of them red socks with the little white logo. Fancied the idea of that.

Then I jumped to my feet, felt I had the right level of booze and went out. In 7—11 I got a batch of bin liners and tape, hailed a passing cab, asked for Clapham. When I got to my house, it was quiet. No police or flashing lights. Turned the walkman up full volume and went in. I dunno how long it took me to bag and tie the bodies. Sweat saturated me and I hummed along to the tapes, keep playing, keep singing. A complete recklessness possessed me. I backed my van up to the front door and just slung them in . . .

"Here we go . . . whoopsy . . . d."

Whoops.

Bit heavy there Dex, puttin' on a few pounds, eh. "Cut out them burgers."

In yah go Lisa.

Yeah . . . make room there Ronnie . . . my man . . . hey
can you stop hugging all the room.

Tight fit guys . . . eh.

Right . . . all squared away.

Everybody happy.

. . . OK . . .

Dex, you'll like this . . . wot Bette Davis said in *All
about Eve*.

"FASTEN YOUR SEAT BELTS. It's going to be a bumpy ride."

I kept up the lunatic stream of banter. Perspiration on
me, my sweat was sweating. The earphones kept slipping
off my head as my ears were drenched. Snatches of Iris
de Ment in and out.

And I kept expecting a neighbour to call the police. But
the street remained silent.

When I'd worked in the nightclubs, we always had a
ton of rubbish. For a few extra quid I'd bring it in the
van and take it to an illegal dump. I drove there now. As
always, there was a line of vans from various Chinese
restaurants and dodgy caffs. No one ever spoke. Dump
yer load and get to fuck and gone. This is what I did now.
Shouted, "Sayonara . . . and don't wait up . . . Garbage ye
were . . . and to garbage ye return."

Got in the van and gunned outa there.

Reclaimed my home. Not that I believed I'd be able to
actually sleep there. How much time before the bodies
were found or for the Roozers to come calling was anybody's guess. But I had a breathing space, didn't have to
fly the Atlantic right now. Time to prepare . . . for wot . . .
anything. I tore off my clothes and spent forty minutes

in the shower. All the soiled clothes, Baldwin's stuff, Lisa's gear, I put in the remaining bin liners and flung them in the van.

Put on a clean pair of jeans, sweatshirt and trainers. I found a batch of notes in Lisa's handwriting and decided to look it over later. I was now sliding into exhaustion and a brutal hangover. Found a half bottle of gin and shoved it in my back pocket and grabbed some music tapes, slammed one in the walkman. Back to the van and eased towards the Elephant and Castle. There's a large container there for unwanted items. I popped the bin liners through the chute. It occurred to me that I could have stuffed Baldwin in easily.

Jeez, how he'd loathe that. The ultimate charity case. Touched the play button and Elvis came blasting: "You ain't nothin' but a hound dog." Elvis took me all the way to Notting Hill. I had a key for the hotel door and went quietly in. The owner was fast asleep on the desk, dreaming of Samarkind perhaps. I dunno why, but I patted him gently on the head.

Slept for fifteen hours and the dreams, wow, a Vietnam Vet would have given his combat jacket to experience. A muddled concoction of:

Baldwin modelling bin liners.
Lisa riding the hotel owner.
Dex attacking me with a needle.
Hearing Elvis singing Rilke.
Coffee cups full of blood.
Garbage dumps peopled by snotty
Shop assistants.
Came to with a shout ...

"Lisa."

And felt awful. Such a benign word, as if you were a touch under par. If there is such a situation beyond despair, apart from death ... that was it.

Next, I looked up to see where I was ... then the money. How many times I'd heard the expression, "Felt like a million dollars."

Don't think that was it. Climbed off the bed and over to the mirror. Would I see a killer of men? No new facial lines. Looked like a ward case ... an old hard case. Checked my watch, evening time. Pulled on the jeans and a shirt, went to reception.

Yup, the owner behind the desk. I said, "Am I a little late for breakfast?"

He smiled and I said, "What do they call you?"

"Jack."

"Jack!"

He looked at my registration card, read, "Noel Murlers . . . so I'm Jack."

"I can see where you might have a point, Jack. OK . . . how about this, rustle up a pot of coffee for us, I'll see you right."

"Most irregular but . . ."

I went back to my room. Five minutes later he came with the coffee and two buttered rolls. I handed him the "Gun" cassette wrapped in a ten-spot. We had clear and dried communication. The coffee gave me adrenaline if nowt else. I moved the rolls and spread Lisa's papers on the bed.

The first sheet read,

> Und dann sinkt ein Leid aug mich, so trube
> wie das gra glanzarmer sommernachte due ein
> stern durchfummert—dann und wann—

Yeah, well, this wasn't very enlightening.

Next up was a travel article on a Spanish town called Ronda. High in the Sierra Nevada. A luxurious hotel there named Hotel Riena Victoria. Looked right out over a stunning cliff top. Situated at the edge was a huge bronze statue of Rilke. Lisa either had . . . or was planning . . . to stay there. As poetic hommage. I don't think she planned on taking me. She'd written,

> Ronda
> [—then,]

As in my dreams
was grey so dark
the people never saw
The sun
over plains, the tarantula stalked
and over
endless games of dice.
The stranger
always lost
in Ronda.
Bandits
grey with rain
who never smiled but
looked annoyed
as nervous
I always paid
and always joked
a foreigner,
who's quickly Spanish,
only provoked
you held your drinks
and drank
another score of gut-red wine.
I think
but held your feet
ignored the barman's coffee
black
mirthless grin
til you got home, sat down
and rocked
your head explode.

Oh, Ronda
in my dreams
I hear your vultures
sweep
below the friendless cliffs
and know I lost
a love insane
beneath your awful cliffs
felt in my mouth
an acid waste
for lovegone lovedied,
all was empty waste

I didn't know what to make of that and said aloud,
"Dunno what to make of that."

Began to hum the Beach Boys, "Help me Rhonda".

Damn tune would be lodged in my head all evening.

Marianne Faithful wrote in her sixties' memoirs, "You
would ask your date, do you know Genet, have you read
a Retours? And if he said yes, you'd hop into bed."

I wasn't about to read Genet, and, course, that was
then. Probably have to read one of those un-spell-able
South Americans now and hint at magic realism. A guy
I knew had wondered why his chat-up line always failed.
He'd tell them he was an arse-shi-tec.

I'd met some of those too.

I wanted the sixties, all that free love passed me by.
Even then I was paying. But I liked the nostalgia for it,
as women love being in love. As I thought this, I thought

I knew what I meant, but I wouldn't have liked to defend, much less define, it.

As I passed reception, I heard a deafening racket . . . and it took a few moments to recognise, "Gun". They hadn't improved in the daylight. Jack was reading, *Reader's Digest*. And said to me, "I study English here. Do you think *is* good?"

"Got me where I am today. I'll be staying a few extra days."

"You are most welcome."

"See, Jack, you've mastered sarcasm already."

I bought a newspaper as I walked down along Hyde Park. No screaming headlines on me yet: on page four, a report said there'd been 46 murders in the first six months of the year. Unlike the cricketers, I managed to bring up half a century. It felt good to walk, the lengthy sleep had helped, and I kept going to Marble Arch. A large pub called The Arch loomed ahead. Now how did they arrive at that name? Music poured out on the path. Marianne Faithful doing her version of "Madame George".

Reckoning this was a stretched example of serendipity, I went in. The place was hopping and I was lucky to grab a stool by the bar. Two tenders. One, a six-foot black with the moves of an athlete. His face resembled Hawk, the sidekick of the Boston P. I. Spenser. If you don't know

him, you're not hurting. I'd like to describe his face as
being touched with acne but . . . it was riddled. What my
old man called "pock-marked". The other tender was a
black woman round about thirty, in there. Black Rules . . .
OK . . . ish.

She'd a lush body that summoned up jail sentences.
Caught me looking or, to be *Reader Digest*ed, I was
"ogling". And she smiled. Jesus, how long now since I'd
had that. A no-frills, no-percentage slice of human
warmth. I'd been in the basement too long.

The guy saw it too and that was less OK. Especially as
he moved to serve me, asked, "See something you like?"

South-London inflection, lots of hard. I could go with
it, said, "Yeah, but guess I'll settle for a drink. A large
Scotch."

"A particular type?"

"Yeah, a wet one."

He let it slide. I could care. The drink came and with
it an appraising look, missing nothing. I wittily said, "And
do you see something you like?"

My eye caught a can with the letters TNT. He picked
one up, said, "Wanna try one, my treat?"

"Pour the sucker."

I took a long swallow. He waited and what else could I
say, so I said it.

"Explosive."

But his eyes were now set over my right shoulder, hard
and concentrated. He said, "Two dudes followed you in
here and they be shootin' glances your way. Now one's
coming over."

"Filth?"

"Naw, the gear is wrong. Those dudes got taste, bad taste but an effect."

I turned and the guy looked familiar. It took a few moments. He said, "Hiya Nick, remember me ... Danny ... from the club."

Yeah, I remembered. Last time I'd met him he'd been calling women "chicks".

"Something I can do for you Danny?"

"Me and George ... that's George, he took over your job when you left. We've been looking for you. Lo and behold, we're cruising round, there you are out for a constitutional. Small world, eh."

He looked at the barman, said, "You wanna park it someplace else nigger."

The barman gave a low whistle and moved down the bar. I said, "So why would you be wanting me Danny?"

"That spade got lifted, Baldwin. He used to know that black piece you've been shafting and, that hard-case Dexy, he knew him. Now it seems the missis paid a mill plus for his return. Me 'n' George, we figger you could help with inquiries, know wot I mean Nick. But hey, we're not greedy, fifty big ones each, we're outa here."

"Go fuck yourself."

Danny sighed. "Not going to happen Nick. George said you'd be difficult. Tell you what, I'll give you a week, say next Friday at your place. How would that suit? Otherwise, as the Yanks say, I'll have to drop a dime on you."

I watched them leave, they waved cheerily. Course my luck was bound to change. I'd hit all the green lights and, when I eased up, luck came and bit me in the arse.

The barman ambled towards me, asked, "Frens of yours?"

"No, I'm real sorry about that crack."

"Wha' dat?"

"Am, you know . . . about you being black."

"Oh, calling me a nigger, dat wot you all want to say."

"I'm sorry. Can I buy you a drink?"

"Yeah, I'll have me a club soda."

"Nothing stronger?"

"That's it. Used to be I was a juicer."

"Excuse me?"

"A dipso, alky, like that. Now I ain't."

"You miss it?"

He passed me another large Scotch, held it up to the light. The gold aura rocked gently and he put it in front of me, asked, "Would you?"

Nursed the drink for a while and thought how I'd miss everything. Then finished it and headed off, shouted, "See you."

He gave a slight nod, nothing elaborate, no fancy show.

As I got outside, Danny appeared right in front, pushed a blade into my groin, said, "Do anything stoopid, you'll be a soprano. Now let's all move down the alley for a wee chat, a business conference, if you like."

We did, if somewhat awkwardly. George was waiting and swigging from a beer bottle. The fucker was big and very little of it was fat. A boxer's ruint face with eyes that never saw the light. What they used to call a nasty piece of work and they were right. As we frog-walked behind him, he gave a huge grin. Yellow uneven teeth, he seemed proud of them. Go figure.

I said, "You're the Colgate nightmare."

And he kicked me in the balls. I'm no different from any other bloke, I dropped and vomited. All thoughts of Rilke, America, life vanished. Howling was the sole ambition.

George said, "Hey Danny, he ain't so tough but I better fix his mouth, wotcha fink?"

Danny thought so too.

He smashed the neck of the bottle against the wall and grabbed my hair, pushed the jagged piece in close to my lips, said, "Time to eat shit hard boy."

I put up my hand and Danny said, "Hold a mo' George."

Near gaggin' on the taste of puke, I managed to say, "Cut me and no cash."

George would have gone for it regardless but Danny knew my form, considered, then said, "Let 'im go George."

"The fuck I will."

Danny grabbed his arm, said, "Don't play silly buggers, you want the readies or not?"

With a disgusted sigh, George pushed me away. I rolled on my side and cupped my groin. Christ, the pain! George spat and said, "Thought you said he was tough, look at 'im, wanking is he?"

Danny bent down, said in a friendly voice, mate to mate, "Nick, watcha say, no harm done, just a misunderstanding, alrite mate. We'll see you Friday, do our bit o' business and yer on yer way. Alrighty, your place, early. Got it?"

I nodded.

George half turned then as if a thought struck him. He lashed out with his foot catching me at the base of my spine, said, "Watch yer back chummy."

Their laughter sounded all the way up the alley.

When I got back to the hotel, I was weak as a kitten.

Showered first and examined my torso, bruises and cuts all over, said aloud, "Shit."

Then climbed into the sack and slept or passed out instantly. I didn't dream, leastways nothing I could recall. Not that I wanted to, my mind was set on horror full.

Woke late evening and my spine was on fire. Eased gingerly out of bed and risked a look in the mirror. Old, a face about to crumble into late middle age, checked my eyes to see if they'd changed. After what I had to do with the bodies, surely it would take its toll. But no difference. I felt randy though. A surge of lust that blocked out the aches. Couldn't believe it, said, "You wanna get laid, is that it. I thought you were all through with women. After Bonny and Lisa, how could you ever bother again."

But my groin said, "Oh yeah, do bother and soon."

Mebbe the action with the needle and the wiggers had unhinged me. A compulsion to talk to myself and out loud was becoming more frequent. Jesus, I'd be one of those sorry bastards who trudge the high street muttering. Well, least ways I'd be a rich one. I'd need to have a plan to deal with Danny and George. I could of course give them the money and pray for a quiet life. Yeah, dream on sucker.

The radio was blaring in the hall of the hotel:

> I went through the desert
> on a horse with no name
> I was glad to come in from
> the rain.

I think that's what I heard. Remember it, one of those songs you heard all the time, you'd no idea what it meant. In fact, if pressed, you couldn't even say if you liked it. But you knew it and, worse, it clung. One of those songs that hung out with, "me and you/and a dog named boo".

I thought of all those half-baked hippies in California smug on soft drugs and sunshine and maybe I'd swing by, hum a mellow tune meself. After Nashville of course. Shit, I had to pay my country dues first.

Checked in the directory for Bill's number. He was the guy who'd given the day's work to Dex and me. The time we moved the furniture and Dex had dealt with the skateboard kid.

Bill was yer London-ed wideboy. The likely lad from the East End. When one of the Krays died, Bill walked behind the hearse. Very few were afforded that privilege. A top CID bloke in step behind. When they showed it on the telly, the huge crowds, you could see Bill as among the lost elite.

I'd known him a long time and once I might even have joined his crew. But, like I said at the outset, I'm not a criminal. Not the obvious sort anyroad. The mix of family and pompous legend was a tad too rich. How many Kray stories can you stomach and then, the exploits of the Richardsons as dessert. No thanks.

Bottom line was, my old man would have shit himself for such a position. I didn't want nuffink he admired. Bill got himself in a bit of stuk a few years back and I helped out. No big deal, no strenuous effort on my part. It appeared more than it was and he believed he owed me. That I played it down only added to its value. How grateful he might still be, well, I was going to find out.

Got him on the line and arranged to meet. In a pub, of course. I needed air, to walk, so headed down Kensington Church Street. The memories began to pound. Then my heart lurched. Here was Lisa walking towards me. Like a physical blow, my heart goose jumped and I staggered back against a railing. Instant sweat stinging my eyes. As she came closer, it was just a young black girl. She gave me a contemptuous look, said, "Sober up mon." I wanted to shout "Why?" But the scare had left me too shaken. Fuck, I hoped I wasn't going to start losing it. Physically, I was strong, always had been but, how do you put muscles on the mind? If it goes soft, how to re-pump it? Was there a gym for it? As if in answer, I looked up and saw the small Carmelite Church on the corner. I knew that 'cos a sign outside read "Carmelite Church".

Remember the old black'n'white movies. The hero is full fucked, all is lost then he looks up and . . . big music score . . . a church steeple. He nips in and an Audrey Hepburn'd nun bathes his face and redemption is found. Nowadays, Demi Moore would have him in the aisle. What's wrong with the picture? Yeah, Audrey Hepburn wasn't in black'n'white films. But, I was confused and cinema vérité wasn't my top priority. I went in and literally took a pew. Jeez, it was so quiet and, yeah, peaceful.

In my old reliable, the maligned *Reader's Digest*, I'd like to read the little items on the bottom of a page called "Points to Ponder". One of them had said: "Never assign more tenderness to a thing than God intended."

Felt someone behind me and whirled round. A tall priest watching me.

I said, "Jesus, don't creep up on a person like that."

"I'm so sorry. I'll work on that if you try not to take the Lord's name in vain."

What is it they call it . . . Black Irish? Dark eyes, dark hair, and swarthy complexion, almost Spanish. And the voice, quiet but, wow, contained and powerful. As if he had to rein it in. He smiled and the warmth was astounding. Some people have that. You get to witness it and you think "Hey, everything's gonna be OK." Would go a treat in the DHSS.

He said, "I'm Father Lee but, we're trying to catch up so, please call me Tom."

"Tom."

"Yes, well it's a bit transparent. I think that the powers that be would like to present us as ecclesiastical game show hosts."

"Big prizes?"

"The biggest. Are you a believer?"

"In game shows?"

"Touché! No, I meant the Catholic faith."

"No. I don't believe in a whole lot."

"Quelle douleur."

"You wot?"

"Nothing. I like to show off. I'd have guessed you weren't a Catholic. You lack a certain servility that gets bestowed early."

He sat in beside me and I said, "You're not a very good promotions man, are you. I mean, is this a sort of inverted sell? Down playing the product to whet my appetite."

The smile again. Jeez, I'd buy that.

"You're a perceptive man. I also think you're a troubled one. Might I be of comfort."

And I wanted to tell him. For fuck sake, I knew him

five minutes and was ready to blurt out the whole sheeb-ang. But got a grip, partially. Said, "I don't think it's really what you've trained for; not in yer curriculum."

"You might be surprised . . . try me."

"Let me ask you this. If a man cares for a person and then causes her death, in a horrible way, does a piece of him die too?"

"You want forgiveness?"

"I want to understand it."

"Go to God."

I stood up and the spell was broken. I gave him a close look and thought . . . "What was I thinking, he's just a bloke in a black suit and a fairly shabby one." I said, "Got to go . . . not to God but Nashville."

He touched my arm and near whispered, "Don't do what you're contemplating, I beg of you."

"Hey, I'm not going to top myself."

"I didn't mean that . . . the other business."

"I'll see you Tom, I've got to leg it. You mind how you go . . . keep the faith, see you again."

Outside I drew some deep breaths; thought he'd said, "I'm afraid not."

I forgot to light the bloody candle and decided I'd burn a whole batch of 'em next time. Shove a tenner in the box, cook up a flaming frenzy. Yeah, I could do that.

The hour was getting on. I had to haul arse to make the pub. Hailed a cab and liked the easy way to travel. I got one in a million. On the glass partition was a large sign, "PLEASE DO SMOKE". I smiled and couldn't miss that the cabbie was certainly setting an example. He was scarcely visible through smoke. True to the taxi code, he was a talker, couldn't shut it. I wonder do the verbals just continue even after the passengers are gone. No mystery to me if they did. Shit, was beginning to enjoy my own rap and I didn't need professional help to figure out where that led.

He was saying, "Yer smoker now, he's the new leper. Know wot I mean John. You got yer politician, yeah, most of 'em got 'er head up their arse, or someone else's more like. They get fat on the tax from tobacco, am I right? And treat the smoker like dirt. I'd a non-smoker get in the cab the other day, started to give me a lecture on passive smoking. Know wot I done?"

I realised he expected an answer, so: "I've no idea."

"Stopped the bleeding cab I did. Told him to hop it, wotcha think of that then."

"Am . . . well done?"

"Too bloody right! Here we are then, Oval tube, right?"

As I paid him, I said, "Keep up the good work."

"Too right I will, the sanctimonious bastards."

And he burned rubber.

The pub was The Greyhound on the corner there, opposite St Mark's. Best grub in South-East London and generous with it. I suppose I better describe Bill. Like Ed Asner with a jig, a hairpiece . . . or how he was in his Lou Grant days. The grouchy-bear effect, the look that says "I'll help you out but don't get fucking notions either." Few did. Most everybody liked him, including me. Dex had said, "He's a wanker."

Perhaps the best endorsement. One end of the pub had the Irish fraternity doing serious damage to rivers of Guinness. Midway was a hockey team, a male one and

they were doing . . . I dunno . . . hockey-ish stuff. The end
alcove had Bill on his tod, such is his rep. I'd heard he
had a baby girl with something wrong. I said, "On yer
lonesome."

"Yeah, makes a change. How are ya Nick?"

"Doing OK."

"Wotcha drinking."

"Scotch."

"Yo' Jimmy . . . couple large Teachers, one for yerself."

We waited till the drinks came, said, "Cheers."

And meant it. Drank deep. Bill wiped his mouth, said,
"I bin hearing about you Nicky. That toe-rag you run
with, Dexy, him and some black bit . . . Mebbe involved
in major bad doing."

"Just talk Bill, no substance."

"Yeah, well, you mind how you go."

"That's why I asked to see you. Do you know two nasty
pieces of work named Danny and George."

He finished his drink and I called for refills, he
answered, "Steer clear of 'em, bad news."

"Not that simple. I need to ask you a biggie."

"You want cash . . . how much and how soon?"

"No, no jeez, I appreciate that."

Then I told him. He was surprised, near shocked but
went with it, said, "That's heavy merchandise, it's gonna
cost."

"I'm good for it."

"When?"

"As soon as."

"OK, gimme two days, then come round my gaff. I'm
not going to stick my oar in but this is serious business."

"It's only for demonstration purposes."

"Do us a favour Nick, alright . . . leave it out."

He got up, said, "So come round in two days, meet my missis and our little girl."

"Yeah, sure I'd love to. Yer little girl, can I bring her something?"

"Sure . . . Alf videos."

"Wot?"

"A cartoon character, she adores him."

"Sure, I'll do that."

He considered a moment, then leant back, said, "We called her Chelsea, give 'er a bit o' class."

"I like it."

"She has Down's Syndrome. Near fuckin' killed me at the time."

I didn't know wot to say, so I said nowt and he continued, more to himself, "Couldn't ask for a spunkier kid. She has more spirit than anyone I ever met. Ain't nuffink she won't try, and a wicked sense of humour. I think I'm the one with the handicap. Anyway, sorry for ranting on. I'll be showing you bleedin' photos next like those sorry fucks you meet on trains. Okey-dokey, I hope you know wot yer playing at."

"Sure I do. Can you locate Danny's home too . . . thanks."

I sat on for another half hour nursing the Scotch. The story about Chelsea really got to me. I dunno why and I sure as hell couldn't afford any extra emotion.

There wasn't music in the pub but these days I was tuned to a continuous internal soundtrack. Iris de Ment lyrics. A song of such loss as most times I skipped it on the album. It's called "Easy" and, of all the things it might

be, easy sure wasn't one of them. As I left, I mouthed the
hook line . . . "and easy's getting harder every day."
    Amen to that.

Next day, I was wound tighter than a Tory, fit to detonate.
Had to do something, get laid mebbe. Decided it might
help and took a wedge from the ransom. Fuck, it seemed
a mountain of cash. No matter how many times I dipped,
it didn't care. I wasn't complaining.
    Headed for Covent Garden. You're surprised, right! You
figured I'd be a Kings Cross punter and sure, I'd been
there, been there lots. But, what's the point of heavy
cash if you ain't going to get heavy action. Same system
though. Go in a phone box and select a card. I was just
off Long Acre and selected this one:

> Trina, South American beauty
> will give you the trip of a lifetime.

Rang the number, got the address and walked round. The
building was flash and I guess I'd be helping with the
rates. An intercom buzzed me through and then I met
the bouncer or pimp or wotever. He was, as Daniel Wood-
rell put it, sixty stitches past good looking. I was going
to share my bouncing credentials but then thought,
mebbe not. There isn't really a brotherhood of bouncers.
Most aspire to be wrestlers on Sky Sports. He said, "Not
the filth, are you pal."
    "No."
    "Yer big enough."
    "But not in the places it matters."

Gave him the money. Enough to fly to Hollywood and collect Alf. Then in to meet Trina. A luxurious pad and "Vienna" playing. She was a beauty and jailbait. Oh yeah, looked about sixteen if you didn't look close. I asked, "You like Ultravox?"

"Excuse please?"

"The group, them singing 'Vienna'."

"Oh I don't know, is spool tape, plays all day. Come in please . . . a drink?"

"Cup of tea, two sugars."

"I don't know."

"Just kidding, any watered concoction will do."

"Whisky."

"Sure."

Handed me that and I took a sip. Yeah . . . tea.

"How can I please you?"

For all the punters, just once to roll it, I said, "No kissing on the mouth, no touching of the hair."

She was lost, so I added, "Look, I'm leaving Old Blighty soon. I'd like one truly memorable fuck before I go."

It was memorable. She put a condom on with her mouth and led me to almost roar YAHOO! But, I'd save that for the States.

Came out into Covent Garden and I was full and proper shagged. The nearest thing to contentment I'd get. A wino asked me for a pound and I gave him a tenner. He shouted after me, "What's the catch?"

Indeed.

Put the house on the market. Told the estate agent I was going abroad and would take a low, low price for rapid sale. I met him at Clapham, showed him over and gave him a spare set of keys. If I could just hold it together, I might make a clean sweep.

The doorbell went. I was wearing the blue suit to blind the estate agent. Opened the door to a near identical one, except the body language shouted COP. He was in his fifties, what they called grizzled. Tufts of steel brillo hair, hard grey eyes. About six foot, he was running to fat but not there yet. Flashed the card.

"Good morning Sir, I'm Detective Brant from the Met, might I have a word?"

"Sure, care to step in."

He did and gave the house a more thorough scan than the property guy.

"Tea, coffee?"

"Coffee—I shouldn't but, my gut is hell and gone anyway. Black with two sugars please."

I got the coffee and motioned him to sit. He glanced round again, said, "Comfortable! And they say Clapham's on the way back."

I often wondered where those areas went in the meantime. The same place as Brant's gut, presumably. Kept these observations mute and waited.

"You are familiar with one Dexter Cole and, lemme check my notebook here—Elizabeth Reed and, yes, Bonny Mellor."

"Did I know them you mean—yes, of course I did. Dex is my neighbour—right opposite in fact, Lisa was his girlfriend and Bonny was my friend."

He gave the procedural puzzled look. I didn't help.

"See, that's my dilemma. Both Cole and Reed have disappeared. Ms Mellor alas was killed in a tragic fire. Your friend you said—but you didn't go to her funeral?"

"I couldn't—too stressful."

"Yes, yes, it would be. In fact, we thought you'd vanished yourself. Bit of a holiday perhaps?"

"Not exactly. I stayed with a friend—a lady."

"And she is?—her address, just for my records you understand. I was led to believe you and the Reed woman were close."

"Naw, she was Dex's piece of skirt. Me, I'm not into black—know wot I mean?"

"I see."

He pondered, then held up his cup. "Might I?"

I was boiling the water when I heard him behind me. Gave me a turn—shades of Dex—but I looked down. He said, "I'm going to level with you Nick."

As no name had been given by me, I was to shake in my boots here. Police psychology one.

"I shouldn't really be divulging this but, perhaps you can help me."

"I'll try."

"A black businessman was kidnapped and we have reason to believe a ransom of over two million has been paid."

The bitch! Upping the ante for the insurance. She'd be lucky.

I gave a low whistle. He said, "Yes, quite a tidy figure, but the man hasn't been released. Our inquiries lead us to believe Cole and Reed might be implicated."

Now I adopted the pondering face, then said, "Might this businessman not have staged it—you know, fake kidnap?"

"Mmm, a possibility, yes—maybe."

"But you don't think so."

He drained the coffee. I was feeling that drained too. He made to leave and said, "If you hear anything about either of those two individuals, please call me. Here's my card. We've reason to believe this Dex character is volatile and unpredictable."

Not any more!

I took the card, made noises of agreement. At the door he thanked me for my co-operation then, looking at my suit, asked, "You're not currently employed Nick, are you?"

Up close our suits were twins. I said, "If I were, would I be wearing this rubbish?"

Next morning I rented a safe deposit box. Not an easy thing to do but persisted. Plonked most of the cash in that and paid for one more week at the hotel. I was getting accustomed to it. Then I got hold of a motor trade magazine and arranged to sell the van. Short of myself, I had near everything up for sale. Whether I'd get to collect any or all of it was the toss of the black dice. Sure beat horse racing though. A whole new slant on the gamblers old cry of—"to make a killing".

Friday was D-Day. The initial could be Danny or worse.

Then the last act. I booked a flight to New York for Sunday—ready to rock and roll.

All day Wednesday I willed myself to relax. Ate three solid meals, exercised, and tried not to project. A huge surge of adrenaline was building and I kept rein on it. Restrain and temper the flow till the hour of confrontation.

On a whim I stopped at a coffee shop and found an empty table. Ordered cappuccino and eased back. The coffee came, frothy and hopping but alas, with company. A couple in their twenties. She asked politely if they could share the table. The guy, in mandatory pigtail, gave me a look. "Not today pal," I thought, "it's my armistice for London time. No way can you piss on my parade."

The guy began a torrent of abuse to his partner. Foul, ferocious, and relentless. I said, "Hey fella, you wanna give it a rest for a bit."

He sneered, something to witness. He was built to maybe burst a balloon—all of the fashionable one-thirty pounds. He said, "This any of your business? You think your bulk intimidates me?"

The girl gave me the pleading stare, the "please don't rile him further" number. So I leant over the table, clamped my hand on his wrist, said, "You want to know what I think? OK—I think you should be very fuckin' intimidated. Now—if you answer me, I'm going to make you eat the ponytail, elastic band and all. See, it *is* my business 'cos you sat at *my* table. So, not a word—shush!"

I drank my coffee and after a few minutes he hepped up and stamped away. She said, "He doesn't mean it."

"But he does—he most certainly does. What I do know is you'll follow him and I dearly wish you wouldn't."

She did.

A new tenant would have been pleased with the bag beneath the bed. They used to say, if you wanted to find a hooker's number, look inside the provided Gideon Bible. Provided you had one. I didn't. Lay on the bed, put on the headphones and let Neil Young sooth me.

> I was wondering what to do,
> and the closer they got, the more those feelings grew.
> Daddy's rifle in my hands felt reassuring,
> he told me RED means RUN son, numbers
> add up to nothing.
> But when that first shot hit the door,
> I saw it coming,
> raised the rifle to my eye, never stopped
> to wonder why.
> Then I saw BLACK and my face flash in the sky.

Hard to figure old Neil had been opening my mail.

As I'd put Lisa into the bin liner, she'd opened her eyes and grabbed my wrist. That terrible rattle was coming from her throat. I'd broken her grip and pounded her down into the bag, a stream of terror pouring from me. Somehow I'd tied the bag but still there was movement. I'd used a shovel to beat down and begged—"for pity's sake, die you bitch"—and came awake.

Drenched in sweat, the headphones still on and ripped them off. It took me a few moments to realise I was whimpering. Crawled from the bed and tore off my clothes, they were sodden with perspiration. Naked, I found the half bottle of gin and gulped at it—my hands could hardly hold the bottle. Even the room was shaking, the death rattle loud in my head. The gin calmed me, it sickened me but my heart slowed down. As did the room. Staggered to the shower and tried to soak away the heebie-jeebies. Said aloud—"thing like that, put a man off sleeping."

Going round to Bill's, I'd

3 Videos of Alf

An Alf doll

Alf T-Shirts

Alf Cutlery

Alf Posters.

Should do it!

To my bitter disappointment, the little girl was out with her mum. I couldn't believe how let down I was. I said, "Ah well, next time."

Bill gave me a look, said, "I don't fink so."

"Wot?"

He handed me an Adidas bag, said, "It's all in there. Danny's address is also innit."

I asked him the price. It was fuckin' steep. I said, "I have a package here which should cover it but lemme add a wedge for your end."

"I don't want your money. We're even now and, if you'll excuse me . . ."

"OK—oh yeah, here's the Alf collection for Chelsea."

He looked at me as if I'd offered him a shit sandwich, said, "I don't think so."

"Hey Bill, don't be such a prick. Where'd you come off bin so high and mighty. You're going to deprive the child 'cos you're suddenly a man of principle—gimme a fuckin' break."

I stormed outa there and was halfway up the road before I realised I still had the bloody toys. I wanted to weep. Of all the things I regret, that might top the list. Passing a litter bin, I dropped them in, my heart in tatters.

Thursday morning I was up at daybreak. Danny's house hadn't been hard to locate, his car outside. Pulled the van alongside and got out, acting as if I'd a flat tyre—even put the wheel up on the jack. Twenty seconds it took. Five minutes later, I was outa there. Jeez, that easy. Now all I had to do was get Danny and George in the car and, as Lauren Bacall said, "Blow." Call it a whim or defiance or plain bloody mindedness, I decided to drop in on the priest, see if he could tell what I'd been at. The church retained the air of quietness but no sign of the priest. I walked up to the altar then spotted an old priest doing church things. Went up to him, said, "Excuse me."

If he was pleased to see me, he hid it well, near barked, "What is it?"

"Sorry to disturb you. I'm looking for Tom—Father Lee."

"No Father Lee here."

"That's Tom Lee."

And feeling foolish, I gave a full description. The old codger glared at me, said, "No priest like that here."

"Mebbe he was a visitor."

"If a priest visited, I'd know."

"But . . ."

"I have a lot of work ahead of me—you must have the wrong church."

"I sure as hell got the wrong priest—no wonder the bloody place is empty."

And I left him to his religion.

Continuing in foolishness, I stopped at a jeweller's and ransomed a gold bracelet. The engraving was included. I know it was a futile gesture but for a moment, it burned bright.

Friday morning I woke early. Did a hundred push-ups, fifty sit-ups, and felt ready. A new Reebok tracksuit and I looked set. Nodded to Jack and strolled down to McDonald's. Ordered their touted breakfast, it had eggs, muffin, sausages, juice. It tasted like absence. And, what on earth do they do to their coffee! An American company, right. But their coffee—like someone had shit in it and never even stirred it. This is not my observation, Dex said it and I thought about him for a bit. When push came to shove, he was found wanting. As Clint Eastwood observed—"you talk too much."

Went to an Italian cafe and got double cappuccino to go. The proprietor asked, "You want I should sprinkle chocolate on the top?"

"Shoot the works."

"That is a fine tracksuit, how much you pay for it?"

"Too much. Can we get on with the coffee."

Got in the van and sipped as I drove to Clapham. When I get there, found a note from the estate agent—he might have a buyer. So I rang him, told him to do whatever and bank the cheque for me. All in place.

They came at noon and I let them in. Danny was wearing jeans and sweatshirt but George had opted for a suit, imitation Armani. I knew enough to know a real one wouldn't bag at the knees. Danny said, "Are we set?"

"Yes, I have the money."

George looked sceptical, asked, "Well sport, where the fuck is it—don't be shy."

"How do I know you'll be satisfied with this payment? Wot's to stop you coming at me again?"

Danny smiled. "But Nick, I give you my word so c'mon, let's see the dosh."

Now I smiled. "What! You think I keep it here in the house. We have to go get it. I have my van, you follow me."

George shook his head. "No, no, no, you come in our motor."

"Then no deal. There's the phone, drop the dime."

Danny signalled to George and they had a heated consultation. Danny won out and my suggestion was accepted. As we went out the door Danny said, "One wrong move and you're fuckin' history arsehole. Am I getting through to you?"

"Perfectly."

I got in the van and drove to Wimbledon Common, took a good hour. I knew they'd be pissed but they kept behind. When we got there I pulled up and watched them stop about five hundred yards from me. I rolled down my windows and signalled for Danny to do likewise. As he did, I banged the horn twice and shouted, "Now, *you're* history arsehole."

The explosion was quite muted but lifted the car about four foot off the ground. The force waves took a second to reach me and shook the van. For a moment I was transfixed then I turned the key and drove the fuck outa there.

I wondered what lines of Rilke would cover this.

The flight to New York left on time. I bought a pair of the red socks and slept through the in-flight movie. A huge amount of money nestled comfortably in the body belts.

After we touched down, it crossed my mind as to how Rilke would translate into American. I was wearing my blue suit and reckoned I looked the part.

They arrested me as I came down the staircase. A small army of uniforms and plain clothes all over. Cuffs were jammed on my wrists as my hands were pulled behind my back. A barrage of instructions roaring back and forth.

"Frisk him—read him his rights—multiple homicide—get his ass in gear."

They took me to Rikers. I felt like an extra in *Hill Street Blues*, but on the wrong side. My pockets were turned out and a small bracelet was found in my top pocket. It had been engraved "CHELSEA".

One of the cops said, "Hey buddy, we kept the Sid Vicious cell vacant for you—where he bought the farm, so you should be right at home."

As I was pushed into a cell, the warden said, "Welcome to The Tombs."

I sat on the bunk and wondered if America was all it was cracked up to be.

Acknowledgements

"Sunday Mornin' Comin' Down"
Words and music by Kris Kristofferson © 1969
Combine Music Corp, USA
Reproduced by permission of EMI Songs Ltd, London WC2H 0EA

"Powderfinger" by Neil Young
Original publisher Silver Fiddle Music
administered by Warner Chappell Music Ltd, 1979

Rilke quotes are taken from
Madness: The Price of Poetry by Jeremy Reed
Published by Peter Owen Publishers, London

"Thunder Road"
Words and music Bruce Springsteen (ASCAP)
© 1984 Bruce Springsteen (ASCAP) for the world
Administered by Zomba Music Publishers Ltd for UK and Eire

Fiction
Non-fiction
Literary
Crime

Popular culture
Biography
Illustrated
Music

dare to read at serpentstail.com

Visit serpentstail.com today to browse and buy our books, and for exclusive previews, promotions, interviews with authors and forthcoming events.

| NEWS | cut to the literary chase with all the latest news about our books and authors |

| EVENTS | advance information on forthcoming events, author readings, exhibitions and book festivals |

| EXTRACTS | read first chapters, short stories, bite-sized extracts |

| EXCLUSIVES | pre-publication offers, signed copies, discounted books, competitions |

| BROWSE AND BUY | browse our full catalogue, fill up a basket and proceed to our **fully secure** checkout - our website is your oyster |

FREE POSTAGE & PACKING ON ALL ORDERS ANYWHERE!

---

sign up today and receive our new free full colour catalogue